BOOK ONE

To speak the name of the dead is to make them live again.

ANCIENT EGYPTIAN PROVERB

Text copyright © 2016 William Meyer
Interior illustrations copyright © 2016 William Meyer

Cover illustration by Gerald Kelley

Sleeping Bear Press™

2395 South Huron Parkway, Suite 200, Ann Arbor, MI 48104
www.sleepingbearpress.com
© Sleeping Bear Press

Printed and bound in the United States.
10 9 8 7 6 5 4 3 2 1

Library of Congress Cataloging-in-Publication Data
Names: Meyer, William, 1979-
Title: The secret of the scarab beetle / written by William Meyer.
Description: Ann Arbor, MI : Sleeping Bear Press, [2016]
Series: Horace J. Edwards and the time keepers ; 1 | Summary:
"After his grandfather mysteriously dies, eleven-year-old Horace
is given a strange gift--a stone beetle. Horace discovers that
he is the heir to an order of time-keeping guardians and finds
himself transported back in time to the ancient
Egyptian city of Amarna"-Provided by the publisher.
Identifiers: LCCN 2015027722
ISBN 978-1-58536-938-6 (hard cover)
ISBN 978-1-58536-939-3 (paper back)
Subjects: | CYAC: Time travel--Fiction. | Inheritance and
succession--Fiction. | Egypt--Civilization--To 332 B.C.--Fiction.
Classification: LCC PZ7.1.M5 Se 2016 | DDC [Fic]--dc23
LC record available at http://lccn.loc.gov/2015027722

To my grandfather, who introduced me to the world of Ancient Egypt,
and to my wife, who gave me the courage to explore it
—Bill

HORACE j. EDWARDS *and the* TIME KEEPERS

the
secret of the
scarab beetle

BOOK ONE

william meyer

PUBLISHED BY SLEEPING BEAR PRESS

CHAPTER ONE

Lying beneath the swing, the right side of his face smashed firmly against the ground, Horace wondered how he'd gotten himself into this mess. For over a month now, he'd managed to go unnoticed—well, at least as much as any new kid could. And that wasn't easy, considering Niles was the smallest town Horace had ever lived in. But now, with Seth looming over him, and Seth's gang of sixth-grade goons ready to pounce, things didn't look good.

Horace tried to slowly push himself off the ground, spitting out a mixture of dirt and twigs. He barely got to one elbow before a second forceful kick sent him sprawling out across the woodchips.

"What d'you think you're doing?" mocked Seth. "Trying to get out of more work?"

Seth was the meanest kid in Niles and also the biggest bully. Horace had routinely watched him trip unsuspecting classmates in gym and even kill innocent squirrels with his slingshot on the playground. And while Horace had done his best to avoid any trouble with him for over a month, this morning, when Horace had refused to let him copy his homework, Seth had lost it.

"Look, look at how Horace is trying to squirm away."

The other boys around Seth were now laughing. Then one of them pressed his foot on Horace's wrist.

"Do you need to use the little girls' potty?"

Horace dared a quick glance to the side, wondering if either Anna or Milton, his two best friends—well, really his only friends since he'd moved—were nearby. But there was no sign of either one. Not even Ms. Shackles, the lunch lady, was in sight, and she constantly patrolled the yard, looking for kids to drag to the principal's office.

"What do you think we should do with him?" one of the other kids asked Seth.

Horace grimaced at the thought of what Seth might have in mind. A sharp pain soon followed as a second shoe—from another boy—pressed down on his wrist.

Seth smirked. "Don't worry. I've got an idea." He reached down and picked up Horace's sketch pad from the ground. It was the one Horace always carried with him to class, and the one he'd been drawing in before getting ambushed on the swings. "Look at all these pretty drawings," Seth said sarcastically.

"Don't . . . don't touch those." For the first time Horace found his voice.

Seth's eyes lit up. "Oh really? Are these *special*?" Seth flipped to another page. "What's this?" It was a drawing of a farm. "Maybe you should have spent more time working on our project instead of these stupid drawings."

Horace was growing desperate, and he began to plead. "I'm sorry, Seth. I'll tell Mr. Petrie after lunch it was my fault. Just leave my stuff alone."

"Too late for that." And with a sharp splitting sound that seemed to tear Horace's insides in half, Seth ripped the drawing in two.

Horace watched the pieces fall to the ground.

"Please, please stop. What do you want from me?"

Seth smiled and tore a second page in half. "I don't want anything, Horace. I asked nicely for your homework this morning, but I guess you were too busy drawing." More pages fell to the ground.

Horace tried to get up again, but Seth's two friends continued to pin him to the ground with their feet. His fingers were starting to turn purple from the pressure.

One of the kids shouted to Seth, "I think Horace is crying!" The other snickered.

Seth threw the remains of the sketch pad onto the ground. "Pick him up."

The two boys stepped off Horace's wrists and yanked him into the air. They pulled his arms behind his back.

"Now, Horace"—Seth was rolling up his sleeves—"I'm going to teach you a little lesson. The next time I want to copy your homework, you better let me. Or else—"

"Or else what? You're going to beat me up, just like you do to everyone else? I'm sure that's going to be really tough with both my arms pinned behind my back. If you're so strong, Seth, why don't you fight me on your own?" Horace didn't know why he said it; in fact, he probably never should have said anything, but it just came out.

Seth started to grind his teeth. Horace had him. It was an unspoken rule of the playground. If Seth didn't accept the challenge, he'd look like a coward, especially since Horace was half his size.

Seth glanced over his shoulder to make sure there still were no adults around. Then he snorted under his breath. "Fine. Let him go. This shouldn't take long." His usually confident voice hinted at the smallest morsel of doubt.

Finally free of Seth's goons, Horace wiped his face clean and pulled a woodchip from his hair. There was no chance he could ever beat Seth in a fight. He knew that. But maybe, just maybe, if he could drag it out long enough, the lunch bell would ring and delay the inevitable for another day.

A forceful shove by one of the kids behind Horace marked the start of the fight. Just inches from Seth's face, he could smell the stench of potato chips and tuna fish from his lunch. Horace stepped back, and within seconds

Seth sent his first punch flying toward his head. By luck Horace dropped his shoulder and felt it graze his right ear. Seth, who never missed and had thrown his full weight into the punch, was surprised by the sudden movement and stumbled forward.

Horace used the extra second to spin around and prepare for the next attack.

This one came higher, and Horace easily ducked again.

Out of the corner of his eye, he could see kids starting to gather in lines by the far doors. He wondered if he just might get out of this mess alive. Probably another minute or two before the lunch bell rang.

Unfortunately, his momentary distraction left him open to Seth's next punch, a powerful uppercut to his stomach. A sucking sound followed as Horace gasped for breath, and the remains of his peanut butter sandwich came rushing into his mouth. He swallowed the acidic mixture and hunched over his knees in pain.

Seth seized the opportunity and wasted no time sending another punch into Horace's temple.

Now Horace's stomach was no longer the only aching

part of his body; the side of his head was throbbing. Through blurred vision he could see Seth readying for the knockout.

But just as Seth cocked his arm backward, one of the other boys called out, "What is *that*?"

"What?" Seth stopped mid-punch, fearful it was Ms. Shackles.

"Look! Up there."

An object was circling above them.

"That's just a bird, you idiot," Seth replied. It let out a sharp cry, a perfectly timed response, but Seth turned back to his wounded victim, angered by the interruption.

"That's not *just* a bird," someone else added. "I think that's a hawk or a falcon."

"What are you talking about? We don't have time for this. The bell is going to ring any second," snapped Seth. "Grab him."

But no one did.

"Watch out!" yelled the boy behind Horace.

"Run!" shouted another.

"What the—" Seth answered in confusion.

The mixture of feathers, screams, and blood that filled the air made it hard to say what happened next. But by most accounts, the final outcome was the same. Seth Davis, the meanest bully in Niles, Michigan, was the one rolling on the ground, while Horace Edwards, the undersized new kid from across the street, stood in a cloud of feathers.

chapter two

News of Horace's feat spread through the school like wildfire. In seven years at Eastside, no one had ever successfully challenged Seth in a fight. Unfortunately, Horace never got much of a chance to enjoy his newfound glory. As quickly as the mysterious bird had dug its talons deep into Seth's arm, Ms. Shackles had swooped Horace up by the collar and dragged him to the principal.

Sitting on the wooden bench outside the office, Horace couldn't stop thinking about the falcon. He had seen the bird circling moments earlier, and the next thing he knew, it was tearing at Seth's arm. Horace had no idea why it attacked Seth or even what it was doing here in Niles.

Falcons were rarely seen in southwest Michigan, and they definitely didn't attack kids on the playground.

"Horace," a voice called from across the hall. The small head of another sixth-grade boy from Mr. Petrie's class peeked around the corner.

"Milton, what are you doing here? If Ms. Shackles sees you, we'll both end up in the office."

The warning did little to stop Milton from dashing across the hall and crouching low next to Horace.

"That was totally crazy! You destroyed Seth. On the way here I saw him crying in the nurse's office." Milton's green eyes were wide with excitement. "So how'd you do it? Did you punch him in the nose, or was it a kick to the gut? I mean, no offense, but you're the same size as me."

Horace just sheepishly smiled. "Honestly, I didn't really do anything. I was barely able to avoid his punches, when a bird swooped down and started attacking his arm."

Milton looked at Horace doubtfully.

"I'm not making it up. This crazy bird came down and went nuts. If it hadn't shown up, I'm sure Seth would have knocked me out cold."

"Wait." Milton paused. "You're serious? A bird?"

"Yeah, I know. It's crazy. I would have loved to beat up Seth, but honestly, Milton, it was a bird."

The sound of voices in the office could now be heard.

Milton peeked over his shoulder. "Listen, don't tell the principal about the bird. He'll never believe you."

Horace smiled back. "Yeah, I guess you're right."

The voice of Ms. Shackles was growing louder.

Milton then reached out and handed Horace a battered notepad.

"My sketch pad!"

"I picked it up after the fight. Some of the drawings are a little crumpled, but I did my best to tape them back together."

"Thanks."

"No worries." Milton raised his fist to bump Horace's. "Good luck."

Milton disappeared around the corner, and another figure was soon by Horace's side.

"Come with me, young man. The principal is waiting." Ms. Shackles's maniacal grin showed off her two missing canine teeth. "And he's not happy."

Horace walked into the principal's office and found himself in a dark, windowless space. There was a plastic plant in the corner, a portrait behind the desk, a framed print on the wall that looked only half complete, and a few knickknacks on the shelf. It smelled of dust, like a used bookstore or an old library. Ms. Shackles motioned for Horace to sit down while Mr. Witherspoon, the principal, finished studying a piece of paper.

"Ms. Shackles, would you please bring in the perpetrator of this act?"

She drew her head back in confusion. "He's right here, Mr. Witherspoon."

Mr. Witherspoon lurched forward in his chair, squinting through his bifocals, his mustache fraying in every direction and his thinning gray hair flapping to the side.

"This young man?" Mr. Witherspoon opened his eyes wide and grimaced slightly at the sight of Horace sitting across from him. Horace's head barely reached the top of the desk.

"Yes." Ms. Shackles's reply was firm.

"I thought you said he was in sixth grade?" He rubbed his jaw slowly.

This made Horace feel even worse.

Mr. Witherspoon twisted his mustache in his fingers and sat back in his chair. "Thank you, Ms. Shackles. You can return to the playground now."

"Are you sure, Mr. Witherspoon? I'd be happy to stay and help." There seemed to be no other job she'd rather be doing than handing out punishments to the students.

"No, that'll be fine. I think we can handle this ourselves."

She flared her nostrils and reluctantly stepped out of the office.

Mr. Witherspoon waited a moment and then turned back toward Horace, clicking his fingers rhythmically on the oak desk. "So, where shall we begin? Let me see here."

Horace could not easily decipher what Mr. Witherspoon was reading under his bushy brows.

"Edwards, yes, Edwards. That sounds so familiar." He paused, and then his eyes widened again as if a light had turned on. "We just registered you for school this summer. You just moved here. Wait a minute—that's right. I remember. Oh my, how did I forget? You're related to Flinders . . . Flinders Peabody. You're his grandson."

Horace blinked in surprise.

Mr. Witherspoon squeezed his chin between his thumb and index finger. "Yes, yes, I see."

But what did he see?

"The eyes are an uncanny resemblance." He paused. "Here, behind me." He picked up a faded photo from the shelf.

Horace leaned in to see a group of three men in the photo. One looked like a much, much younger version of Mr. Witherspoon (eyebrows as unkempt as ever). The second, Horace had never seen before, but there was no doubt about the third. It was his grandfather.

With Mr. Witherspoon's encouragement, Horace looked closer at the photo and saw his familiar resemblance to his younger grandpa, but it wasn't the eyes. It was his hair; it was sticking straight up.

"Your grandfather and I used to travel all over the world

when we were younger." Mr. Witherspoon let out a loud laugh. "There was nothing Flinders couldn't find." He smiled. "Not even your grandma could escape his pursuit."

He let out another laugh. "Yes, that was a long time ago, though," added Mr. Witherspoon, half to himself. "My, how things have changed."

It was weird to think of Mr. Witherspoon traveling, or being anywhere besides school. Horace never really thought about teachers or principals *not* being in school, as if the school were the only place they existed.

"Now, how could Flinders's grandson find himself in any sort of trouble?" Mr. Witherspoon asked with a trace of sarcasm.

Horace wasn't sure where to start. Should he mention the bird? Milton had made it pretty clear that was a bad idea. He began carefully, "Well, I was out on the swing when another kid came up to me."

"Seth . . . Seth Davis. Right?"

"Yes."

"He's the one you attacked with your nails? Brutish act, brutish act."

Horace now realized what Ms. Shackles had told Mr. Witherspoon.

"Well, Seth came up to me when I was on the swing, and challenged me to a fight."

"A fight?" Mr. Witherspoon paused, weighing the truth of Horace's story.

Staring at the dust that had gathered at the base of the picture frames, he couldn't bring himself to look anywhere near Mr. Witherspoon's eyes, or his eyebrows, for that matter. It was starting to feel like a giant spotlight had turned on him. He continued, the words in his head swimming again in circles. "He . . . He pushed me to the ground."

"Really?" Mr. Witherspoon's voice showed growing doubt. "And then?"

Horace wasn't sure how much longer he could drag things out without mentioning the bird. If there was one thing Horace was really bad at, though, worse than math, even, it was lying.

The phone rang, and they both looked down at Mr. Witherspoon's desk.

"Oh, I hate getting interrupted." Mr. Witherspoon scowled. "This thing never stops ringing." He stuck his head out the office door. "Ms. Neely, will you please take a message for me?" He turned back toward Horace. "Where were we?"

Horace was about to resume the story, when he started coughing. Ms. Neely suddenly appeared in the doorway, her floral perfume wafting in ahead of her.

"Yes?" Mr. Witherspoon asked in frustration.

"I'm sorry, but the caller says it's important."

"Important?" He paused, and his eyebrows twitched just slightly.

"I'm afraid it's Mrs. Edwards, Horace's mother."

Mr. Witherspoon scratched his brow. He looked just as confused as Horace did now.

"I'd better answer it." He reached down and picked up the phone. "Hello?" A short pause. "Oh no . . ."

Horace was staring at the phone and trying to catch his breath.

"I have him right here."

How did his mom know about the fight already?

"Yes, I think it's best you take him." Mr. Witherspoon looked at Horace and then put the phone down. "Horace, we need to get your stuff. Your mom's coming in a few minutes to pick you up."

Horace didn't know whether to be happy or terrified. Mr. Witherspoon seemed to have completely forgotten any thought of punishment or detention. But if his mom were coming to punish him instead, it would certainly be worse than anything Mr. Witherspoon had in mind.

As they walked into his homeroom, seventeen kids sat in stunned silence, an unusual scene from the daily bustle of the class.

Mr. Witherspoon motioned to Mr. Petrie to meet him at the door and told Horace to get his things. His old teachers in Ohio had loved to hang stuff from every nook and cranny, but Mr. Petrie's room had a much simpler style. Perfectly laid out, the bulletin board had little quotes stapled around its edges. A row of evenly spaced markers lay beneath a spotless whiteboard.

Horace collected his books from his desk. Anna, who sat in the seat next to his, leaned over. "What happened?

Where's Seth? Milton said they had to call an ambulance to take him to the hospital," she whispered.

Horace just shrugged. He didn't have an answer.

"Are you in trouble?" Anna asked. Her face was bright red, which was, coincidentally, also the color of her hair and the bands on her braces.

He didn't have an answer for that, either. He didn't know what was going on. But he looked around the room and saw Seth's desk was empty too.

"Wally got a week's detention last year for clogging all the sinks in the bathroom with paper towels, but I can't imagine they would do that to you. You're new." She tried to comfort him.

Horace was hoping to avoid his other classmates' stares and any more of Anna's questions. He quickly approached Mr. Witherspoon and Mr. Petrie. They immediately stopped talking.

"Don't worry about your homework tonight," said Mr. Petrie. "We can catch up with your writing later." Horace was surprised by the change in his teacher's tone. For most of the morning Mr. Petrie had been furious with Horace and Seth for not finishing their homework the night before, but now he was being nice.

Out of the corner of his eye, Horace saw Milton smiling from ear to ear and giving him a thumbs-up. Then another boy started clapping. Soon the whole class was cheering and shouting Horace's name. Horace couldn't believe it. Neither could Mr. Petrie.

"What is going on? Stop it! Stop it or there will be no gym this afternoon!"

Horace didn't hear what happened next because Mr. Witherspoon took him back down the hall. The bird attack, the phone call from his mom, and now this—the whole day had been so strange. Nothing like this had ever happened to Horace. He didn't even get to go home early when he sprained his arm at recess in first grade.

As they reached the front doors, Horace's excitement faded. He immediately knew something was wrong when he saw his mom. Her rusty red station wagon was parked right outside, and two dark circles framed the bottoms of her eyes.

She took Horace's bag off his shoulder. "I'll meet you

in the car, Horace. I have to speak with your principal."

"Okay." Horace shrugged.

As he walked over to the station wagon, his mind started racing at the sight of his two older sisters sitting in the backseat. "What's going on?" he asked.

Lilly just sat staring out the window. She wasn't at all like her usual chatty self. And Sara, the oldest of the three, looked equally as confused.

Horace looked between the two of them. "So . . . why are you here?"

"We don't know," Sara finally answered. "Mom won't say."

After a few more minutes of talking with Mr. Witherspoon, their mom walked to the car and opened the driver's door. She placed Horace's bag next to her on the empty passenger seat but said nothing. This didn't feel like it was about the fight. And when she turned left out of the school parking lot and drove past their house without even a side-glance, it suddenly hit Horace: They weren't going home. They were heading to the farm.

chapter three

Horace bit down on his lip, totally confused why they were heading to his grandparents' farm. He hadn't been out there since school had started.

When he had first moved to Niles over the summer, Horace used to ride his bike over to his grandparents' every day. He would work side by side with his grandfather, sometimes planting flowers, other times helping around the house. While they'd work, his grandfather would talk about his travels throughout the world, and sometimes even about his adventures from the past. Horace would fall asleep at night dreaming about all his grandpa's stories, and the next morning, if he could get to the farm early enough, he'd arrive to the sound of sizzling bacon and the smell of buttery pancakes. There was no place on a summer day he'd rather be.

Lilly and Sara had very different opinions about the farm, though. They insisted the whole house was haunted, full of secret passages and hidden rooms. According to the two of them, Niles was part of the Underground Railroad, and their grandparents' farmhouse was one of the first stops in Michigan. Lilly, who almost never visited the farm anymore, said there were probably tons of ghosts roaming around the place.

The sound of gravel under the tires awoke Horace from his thoughts. He could see the black shutters and whitewashed brick of the Victorian farmhouse. Behind the house stretched a sea of endless fields. In the midst of all the corn towered an impressive sycamore tree. The lone tree seemed to predate everything on the farm.

Horace's uncle was waiting at the door and nodded at their car as it rumbled up the drive. He was a real estate agent in Niles. Last year he'd sold more houses than any other person in the county and had been named Realtor of the Year. Everyone always raved about what a nice guy he was. There was something about his droopy eyes and his overenthusiastic laugh, though, that Horace didn't quite trust, no matter how many houses he sold or birthday gifts he gave.

Two cars were parked next to the garage; both were from the Niles police.

His mom turned off the engine and scanned their faces in the rearview mirror. "I want the three of you to stay in the car." With that, she got out.

The exchange among the police, his uncle, and his mom lasted only a few minutes. One of the men was Milton's father—they had the same deep dimples and dark skin—but he was twice Milton's size. The name Williams was written across a patch on his shirt. Soon Horace's mom was walking toward the car, and Officer Williams and his uncle were heading to the rear of the house.

"Are we going home?" Sara seemed confused by their mom's quick return and decision to squeeze into the backseat with them.

"No." His mom paused. "I have to tell the three of you

something." An audible strain was growing in her voice. "Last night there was a break-in at the house, and"—she began to choke up—"in your grandfather's struggle to stop the intruder, he had a heart attack. Before the ambulance could arrive . . ."

Horace's mouth started to go dry.

"He died."

Sara slumped down in her seat.

"You're lying!" Lilly shouted.

Horace fell into a silent shock. A break-in? His lungs suddenly tightened; his hands lost all sense of feeling. Dead? He closed his eyes and squeezed, hoping to push out the word. What did she mean a break-in? How could his grandpa be dead? He was fine. He was alive. Tears started to run down Horace's face.

His mom reached out and grabbed the three of them in a firm hug. Horace still couldn't wrap his mind around it. Niles was boring, and maybe a little weird, but he hadn't thought it was dangerous.

There was something else deeply unsettling about the news. It seemed to awaken a memory tucked into the recesses of his mind. His grandpa was always worried about security. He'd often ask Horace if he remembered to lock the door, or if someone knew where he was going. None of it ever made any sense to Horace, since the farm was the quietest place in Niles, and Niles might well be the quietest place on Earth.

It felt like an hour, but it could have been five minutes before his mom finally loosened her grip. His sisters gazed unblinking out the windshield, still in shock, as Horace wiped his eyes with the end of his sleeve.

"I need . . . the three of you . . . to be strong." His mom collected herself and looked at them. "No one expected this, especially not your grandma, but there are things we have to take care of before we can go home. And I need each of you to help." Horace could have sat in the car for the rest of the day, but he knew his mom meant it. They needed to be strong, not just for their grandma but for their mom, too.

As they slowly got out of the car, he noticed a piece of yellow police tape hanging across the porch. Muddy footprints littered the white floorboards, and two wooden posts were snapped at the base. At the far end of the front porch was a broken windowpane, and on the lawn a series of burnt marks in the grass.

His mom lifted the tape so they could walk under it.

The whole house looked as if it had been turned upside down and shaken violently. Mail had been strewn across the floor, and furniture was everywhere. A pile of broken glass littered the floor, and a clock dangled by a single nail on the wall. Even the hallway, which he remembered having been meticulously lined with antiques and old photographs, was now almost impassable.

His mom stepped over a stack of books and turned toward the three of them. "Sara and Lilly, I need your help upstairs. And, Horace, I need you to watch Grandma. We'll be right back." She pointed at the rocking chair in the living room.

His grandma held a pair of knitting needles in her hands, and her silver hair glowed in the afternoon sun. Through the window, Horace could see his uncle and Officer Williams outside, still walking around the yard.

Over the last two years his grandma had started to

change. Her eyes had dimmed, her laughter wasn't as loud, and her memory was no longer sharp. She had also become a little feisty, too. At Thanksgiving she accidentally cooked an empty tray in the oven for three hours, leaving the whole family with a turkey-less dinner. The doctor explained that these were all signs of early-onset dementia, a disease that made its victims lose their memories one by one.

Horace began to carefully navigate past the upended wooden chairs and pillows strewn across the floor. The living room looked even worse than the entry, with its smashed furniture and scattered papers. He finally reached the couch after high stepping a pile of glass, this one from a knocked-over reading lamp.

It was hard to tell if she was asleep or awake.

"Grandma?" he said in his softest voice. "Grandma?" he repeated, this time a little louder, but still afraid to startle her. He bent over and could see her eyes were open. She was staring blankly out the window at the yard.

"Grandma, it's me, Horace."

It was subtle, but he was certain this time she had moved.

"Grandma, are you okay?"

She blinked again, recognizing his voice, or maybe his words.

There was a quilt on her legs. He pulled it up over her frail shoulders.

"Can I get you something? A glass of water?" He was about to walk over to the kitchen, when she started speaking.

"Horace." Her voice was warm, just like always, but underneath was an almost unnoticeable quaver. "Thank goodness you're safe."

His first thought was about the fight. But how did she know about the fight with Seth? He reddened in embarrassment.

She continued. "They found us. I don't know how, Horace, but they found us."

Suddenly the afternoon sun fell behind a thick cloud, and the room was covered in darkness. This wasn't about the fight.

"Who, Grandma?"

His grandma's stare became more distant and her words even more cryptic. "It doesn't matter. What matters is that you're safe. You must find the key."

Now Horace was the confused one. He anxiously bit down on his lower lip, a habit he'd formed whenever he got nervous. "What? What key?" He wasn't even allowed to lock his bedroom door.

"The key. You have to find the key. The one that opens our secret door."

"What are you talking about, Grandma?"

But his grandma ignored his question. "You're the only one who can help. Find the door, and you will find the boy. Help him before it's too late." For the first time she stared directly at Horace with an intensity he hadn't seen in years. "Promise me, Horace. Promise me you will find the key and help the boy."

After a long moment of silence, he answered, "I promise."

chapter four

The conversation with his grandma had been cut short by his sister's arrival. Lilly had found an amethyst upstairs and, in the excitement of her new charm, it seemed like she had forgotten all about their grandfather's death. But not Horace. He couldn't stop thinking about his grandpa or his grandma's cryptic message. What did she mean by "a key"? Where was there a secret door? And who needed help?

The sun was low on the horizon by the time they got home. Horace made his way up to his bedroom, too tired to eat and too sad to do any of his schoolwork. He collapsed on the edge of his rumpled bed. It had been a long day, and for a while he just stared out the window, in a daze. He probably would have eventually fallen asleep then and there had it not been for a sudden knock on the door.

"Come in." Horace's voice was quiet.

His dad stood in the doorway. He was an accountant and still wearing his suit from work. While he usually greeted Horace with a smile and a hug, tonight was different. His eyes, usually two beacons of light, were dim and red-rimmed.

He joined Horace on the edge of the bed. "I know you're sad. We all are."

Horace just sat there, scratching his thumb against his index finger. It took too much strength to answer.

"It's been a tough day." His dad began to rub Horace's back. "You and your grandpa were lucky to spend so much time together this past summer."

Horace tried to recall his grandpa's voice. *Look at this, Horace. Can you believe that? Wow!* His grandpa was so excited about everything. He wasn't like anyone Horace had ever met. To him, the world was a wonderful adventure, ready to be explored. And the past—he loved the past. It wasn't just about some facts to be memorized or some bones to be dug up; with his grandfather's stories, the past was alive. His grandpa's favorite place was the museum he had worked at in Niles. He took Horace to exhibits on the Potawatomi Tribe and the other Native Americans who had first lived in Michigan. He'd even shown him the famous two-headed lamb, the pride of the whole collection.

One memory stood out above all the others, though. It was toward the end of the summer, only a little more than a month ago. One afternoon, Horace had ridden his bike over to the museum to help his grandpa. The two of them ended up climbing the old turret at the top of the Chapin Mansion, the historic house that held the main collection. From the window, they could see the entire town. His grandpa pointed out all the buildings, telling stories of their past and naming some of the famous people who lived in them. He was so excited to have his grandchildren living in Michigan now. "You know," he said in his gentle way, "you have an important name too, Horace, one connected to Niles's most famous resident."

"Who, Grandpa?"

"Horace Dodge. The same man who started the Dodge car company with his brother, John. It was here where they had their first idea for a car." He pointed toward a water tower in the distance. "That's where they lived." He then turned and smiled. "You never know what great things you'll find here in Niles."

At the time Horace had felt so much possibility sitting there above it all, but now there was no future—or at least not an exciting one without his grandpa. And nothing new to discover in Niles but sadness and grief.

Sensing Horace's growing despair, his dad squeezed his shoulder. "See those?" Dad asked, pointing at the glow-in-the-dark stars on the ceiling. "Your grandfather may have left us, but I promise you, he is watching and guiding you from heaven now. You only need to stop and listen to hear his voice."

There was something about his dad's words Horace knew was true. A piece of his grandfather was still with him, even though he was no longer alive.

"I know it's hard for you to hear, Horace, but this, too,

will pass in time. Everything changes in time, even these tough moments. Out of them will grow something good." His dad gave him a soft kiss on the forehead. "Now why don't you try to get some sleep?"

Horace was still in his school clothes, but he didn't have the energy to change.

His dad pulled the sheets up to Horace's neck and turned off the lamp. "I love you."

"I love you too, Dad." He knew his dad was trying his best. It wasn't easy for any of them.

Just as Horace was drifting off, a strange and hushed conversation made its way up through the vent next to his bed. He'd often overheard his parents talking late at night, usually about money, but this conversation was different.

"I know it's hard to believe, but that's what the police report stated," his dad said.

"This wasn't a robbery, Jack," his mom insisted.

"You just have to let the police do their job," his dad replied.

"There's more to the farm than anyone realizes."

"There's nothing out in those fields, Liz. Those were

just bedtime stories your dad told you when you were kids."

Horace pushed his ear against the cold metal of the vent.

"Why do you think the police can't find any evidence? A fingerprint, a piece of hair, nothing? I'm telling you, this wasn't a random robbery, and he didn't die of a heart attack."

"Well, if it wasn't a heart attack that killed him, then what do you think it was?"

The sound of running water drowned out his mom's answer.

Lilly was brushing her teeth. She always ruined things!

By the time the faucet had stopped running, the conversation was over. He'd missed it. All he had were bits and pieces.

A deep chill filled his bones. What was his mom saying? His grandpa hadn't died from a heart attack? The thought was overwhelming. What could have happened to his grandpa?

It would take another hour before sleep finally came.

When he opened his eyes, he was back at his grandparents' farm. In the distance, he heard a great rumbling sound, almost like the roar of a lion. A storm was coming. Horace could see the wind passing over the fields, and then it hit the tree in the backyard with a blast of fury. The limbs came to life, thrashing back and forth as if fighting against some unseen force.

He reached down and clutched at the grass to keep from being blown away. But when he finally looked up again, he realized the tree wasn't there anymore. In its place was a giant pillar. A single slab of towering stone. But it was starting to wobble.

A voice called out, "Horace. Horace, help me."

It was coming from inside the house.

Horace started to run toward the house as fast as he could. The front door was open.

"Help me, Horace," the voice repeated.

Horace ran through the front room.

"Horace," the voice repeated. It was coming from the second floor.

Horace ran up the stairs and onto the landing. The hallway was much longer than he remembered. And instead of three doors, there were a dozen. But each time Horace opened a door, he found an empty room. He started running down the hall. The slamming of doors drowned out the echoes of his feet on the wood floor.

"Horace," the voice continued to call, even more desperate than before.

Horace's heart was pounding. Another door, and another. Horace opened each one faster than the last, shutting them harder and harder. Sweat was pouring down his face as he finally reached the last one and swung it open.

It was his grandfather's office. But the only thing inside was a clock. A grandfather clock.

Horace jumped upright in his bed. He could hear the clock on the first floor of his house. It was three in the morning. He had had bad dreams before, but nothing like this, nothing so vivid. He got out of his bed and changed into his flannel pajamas. Then he quietly made his way over to the bathroom to get a drink of water. It was a little trick his dad had taught him to get rid of nightmares. After he finished drinking from the cup, he walked into the hallway. He was starting to feel better, when he heard a clicking sound coming from his room.

As he walked toward the door, he realized the sound was coming from the window. It was a bird. A falcon—the one from the playground! It was hovering outside, pecking at the glass. Was he still dreaming?

There was a loud bang as the bird flew hard into the window. It wanted to get inside! Another bang, this time louder.

"Stop," he whispered as he rushed toward the window. "You're going to wake everyone up." In desperation, he pulled the lower window frame open, hoping to scare the creature away.

Without hesitation the bird swooped in and circled his head. Feathers were falling everywhere, and the three model planes hanging from the ceiling were swinging violently on their fishing line. Horace ducked under his desk as the bird dive-bombed in repeated circles. He tried meekly to swat at it with a comic book, but this only aggravated it more. It let out a high-pitched screech and snapped at his fingers.

He turned around to make another last swipe at the bird, but to his amazement it had flown back out the window.

As quickly as it had appeared, it was gone. Horace popped up from under the desk and reached to shut the window, when he stopped short. There, beneath the window, wasn't the bird, but the unmistakable silhouette of a man.

Horace jumped back in shock.

He gathered up his courage and peered out the window again. This time the lawn was empty. Did he imagine that, too?

He didn't have time to worry about it now. There was the sound of approaching footsteps coming from the hall. He dropped the comic book he'd been holding onto the desk and dove into the safety of his bed, and not a moment too soon.

His dad stepped into the room and mumbled something under his breath then walked across the room and shut the open window. Horace lay there and held his breath. It seemed like forever before his dad finally closed the door again. Then he was alone.

chapter five

The next morning Horace awoke to the sound of his alarm. He blinked slowly, head lolling to the side, before slipping back under the sheets and onto his pillow. He actually felt a little better from the night's sleep. There was nothing to worry about, he told himself. It was all just a bad dream.

As he rolled over, his sketch pad at the foot of the bed fell, and the sudden thwack startled him. He peered out from under the sheets at the notebook and noticed a handful of feathers scattered across the room. Two of his model airplanes were dangling overhead by a single string, and the third plane was upside down.

"Breakfast!" a voice called up the stairs.

Horace popped out of bed. What was he going to do? Should he tell his parents about the bird and the strange man?

He started scurrying around the messy room, collecting the discarded feathers.

"Breakfast!" the voice called again.

Horace threw the feathers into the trash bin, brushing off any remaining ones from his pajamas before walking down the rickety front steps. At the foot of the stairs sat Archimedes, the family cat. More than once, Archimedes had taken a snap at Horace's fingers when he'd tried to sneak into his sisters' bedroom to use their computer. The shaggy gray mass stared at Horace and let out a warning hiss as he passed.

"Horace, are you going to school like that?" Sara asked, looking apprehensively at his hair as he sat down. "And what are those feathers doing in your hair?" She plucked one from behind his ear.

"Thanks," he said meekly.

Lilly pulled the earbuds of her phone out and jabbed

them at Horace. "Seriously, you look like you got in a fight with Archimedes last night. Do something with your hair, Horace."

He quickly shook his head, trying to free the last of the falcon feathers before his mom noticed. Lucky for Horace, she was preoccupied with getting everyone's lunches ready for the day. "Can one of you go get some chips for your lunches from the basement?" his mom asked.

Sara got up and headed down the stairs. Horace let out a quiet sigh of relief and returned to eating his cereal. He hated the dark and especially the basement. Lilly knew it. In fact, it was mostly her fault. When their mom had let her babysit, she used to keep Horace up late at night watching scary movies about blood-sucking vampires and flesh-eating zombies. And all Horace could remember was the fact that every one of them seemed to live in the basement.

Lilly went back to her music, and the next few minutes were more or less silent, at least by his family's standards. Horace wondered if this was his chance to tell his mom about the strange events from last night. But before he ever got a chance, the silence of the kitchen was broken by another sound: the ringing of the phone.

"Hi, honey," his mom answered.

Pause.

"Oh, not again . . ."

There was another pause, this time much longer than the last.

"Really . . . All right, I'll be there in ten minutes." She hung up abruptly.

Sara emerged from the basement, carrying three bags of chips. "Who was it, Mom?" She seemed to sense a shift in their mom's demeanor.

"Your dad." She scanned the kitchen. "He forgot his briefcase and wants me to drop it off this morning."

"But you said you would drive me to school today! I've got to carry all my stuff for soccer," pleaded Lilly.

His mom paused, and for a moment Horace thought she would stay and he could still tell her, but then she grabbed their dad's briefcase off the counter. "I can't. He needs it for a meeting."

Horace stared across the table. It looked like Lilly

might start crying.

"Sara will be with you. And you can walk to school." She turned toward Horace. "Just don't cut through the neighbor's lawn." She forced a smile. "I'm sorry, but I have to go." She hesitated and then tried to reassure them. "Don't worry. I'll take you later in the week. There's just a lot we have to deal with right now."

Before any of them could protest, their mom slipped out the door.

Suddenly Sara realized she was in charge and started barking out orders.

"Now, Lilly, get your lunch out of the fridge and put a sandwich in Horace's bag. Horace, go upstairs and change." She put her hands on her hips. "I'm not getting in trouble because of you two."

"Don't tell me what to do," protested Lilly. "You're not Mom!"

"You heard me!" shouted Sara. "Get the sandwiches and let's go."

When he reached his room, Horace slipped out of his pajamas and into his school clothes. He could hear his sisters packing their bags at the front door. It was getting late.

"Horace! We're not waiting for you."

He went into the bathroom to brush his teeth. He put down his toothbrush and walked into his room, searching for his backpack, when he heard the loud slam of the screen door. So his sisters really had left.

While he was reaching for the tattered strap of his backpack, he heard a knock at the front door. Sara and Lilly were starting to drive him crazy.

Another knock. "I'm coming, I'm coming."

As he reached the bottom step, he looked up. A very large man stood in the doorway, holding a small brown package with a bright-red wax seal.

"Mr. Edwards."

For a minute Horace tried to convince himself the man was a delivery guy and just wanted his dad. "My dad's not here. He's at work. You could try coming by later if you want to talk to him. Or you could try his office in town," Horace added, attempting to be polite.

"Mr. Horace j. Edwards."

Horace stepped back. No one ever called him by his full name. In fact, few people even knew it. He'd once asked his mom what his middle initial stood for, and she gave him some confusing explanation about a nurse and a mistaken pen mark. He didn't really believe her or bother to ask again, but over the years it had become their secret signal she'd sometimes use when she left him notes.

Horace gazed at this broad-shouldered man and instantly recognized his shape from the night before. This was no deliveryman! It was the stranger on the lawn!

Horace reached out to slam the door.

The wood made a sharp cracking sound as it crunched against the man's foot. His shoe was already inside the threshold. Horace was about to make a dash for the kitchen phone, when the stranger suddenly reached out and grabbed his wrist. Horace pulled with all his force, but his arm remained locked in the man's firm grip. Out of the corner of his eye he now noticed the glint of a second object. The small package was on the ground and had been replaced by a knife.

"Help" was the last word Horace managed to get out,

just before everything went black.

"Horace, Horace, wake up, Horace."

He blinked. "Dad."

"Horace. Horace, wake up."

"Dad, is that you?"

But the deep voice wasn't his dad's. And as Horace blinked again, he made out the broad-shouldered man looming over him.

His whole body twisted in a violent convulsion as he tried desperately to pull away. But his strength was nothing compared to this grown man's grip.

"I'm so sorry," the man said as he lifted Horace to his feet. "Rules of the Order."

Horace started patting his chest and examining his body for blood. The knife had only nicked his index finger. It was no worse than a paper cut. He was alive.

"What . . . What do you want from me?"

As if things couldn't get any stranger, a second shape swooped down from a tree. To Horace's surprise, the man just stood there as the falcon landed on his outstretched arm.

"You know this bird?" Horace asked hesitantly.

"Shadow and I have been trying to get your attention these last couple of days."

Horace just stood there in stunned silence.

"She can sometimes be temperamental, but she really means well." As if reading his mind, the strange man answered. "I'm so sorry. I know you must have many questions. I guess I didn't need to get the knife out before I even introduced myself. I've always been bad at formalities. Let me start over." He bowed deeply. "My name is Herman, and this here is Shadow." The bird squawked. "We've been sent to deliver this package to you."

Horace bit down on his lip. He still wasn't sure if he should try to make a break for it. But if this Herman guy had really wanted to hurt him, he could have easily done it by now.

"It's for you." Herman looked over his shoulder. "I'm so sorry, but we don't have a lot of time."

"For me?" Horace asked innocently.

"Yes"—Herman smiled—"you."

Horace walked out into the sunlight and got a much

better look at Herman. He wasn't nearly as big as he had first appeared, nor was he as tough. It could have been the way he stood, his arms by his sides, or how his broad shoulders blocked the morning sun, but Herman looked a lot like his grandpa, just a little wider and younger. He had specks of gray scattered throughout his knotted hair, and even a few wrinkles. If Horace didn't know better, he'd have said some of the lines on Herman's face even looked like scars.

"Horace, I need your hand again," Herman said contritely. He held Horace's index finger over the package until a small drop of blood fell onto the seal.

What followed was even more bizarre. The seal, which resembled a bird's eye, started to melt, and the brown paper around the package grew dark. It seemed to be burning from the inside out. The package glowed and then hissed. And there, finally, in Herman's palm, covered in a pile of ash, was what looked like a small, blue stone in the shape of a beetle.

CHAPTER SIX

"Grandma! Grandma, I think I found it!" Horace had waited all day to say those words. After the encounter with Herman, he'd considered skipping school entirely to go directly to the farm, but he decided the risks were too great.

He'd come to the farm with the hopes of showing his grandma the beetle and finding answers to his pressing questions. But now, as Horace stood there, his certainty and excitement were gone. The dangers were very real; Herman had made that clear. And Shadow had flown above him the whole day as his new companion and guardian. She had circled over the playground to all his classmates' delight and had even scared away the neighbor's dog as

Horace had ridden his bike to the farm.

"Grandma!"

No cars were in the driveway, no rockers on the front porch, not a single light in any of the windows. His bike and backpack lay on their sides next to the gravel driveway.

Without warning, a tear streamed down Horace's face. There was so much he wanted to say, so much he wanted to know. Not just about the beetle or the secret door. He wanted to ask his grandma about his parents' conversation the previous night, the Order Herman had mentioned, and, of course, what had really happened to his grandpa. The questions were overwhelming and so was the feeling of loneliness spreading through his whole body. His grandma wasn't here and neither was his grandpa. Horace began to cry.

A few minutes passed before Horace was able to gather himself and gain control of his emotions. He wiped his face with his sleeve.

"Grandma!" he yelled one last time, desperate for a reply.

If there was more to the farm, he was going to have to find the answers on his own. He rubbed his eyes again before reaching into his pocket. A dirty tissue fell out. He searched a little more, found a handful of quarters, and then, there at the bottom, grasped the beetle. There was something reassuring about having the small stone in his hand.

He searched under the flowerpot next to the door and found the key his grandparents had hidden. The lock on the front door clicked open with a simple turn and he started walking around the house, exploring the ins and outs of the first floor. Past the bust his grandpa kept in the foyer, through the kitchen with its wooden cupboards and stuffed pantry, and finally around the living room. Twice Horace walked the same path, wondering if there really were any secret latches or hidden panels in the old house. The second floor was even less promising as Horace looked through his grandparents' room and then the guest bedroom without discovering a single clue or even the smallest hint of a secret door. Finally, as he was starting to lose hope, he walked into his grandfather's office.

The afternoon sun shone on the worn floor panels, and there was a pile of papers on the desk by the window.

Horace made his way past the bookshelves to the desk. On top was a map of Niles. He flipped through another set of drawings and discovered an even older map. This one was of Detroit. Finally, beneath all the pages was a crumbling image that stretched across the whole desk. It felt brittle to the touch, like a dried leaf that had fallen from a tree. However, unlike the other maps, drawn down the middle wasn't a street or a railroad line but the unmistakable shape of a river. Next to the river was a single word: *Nile*. But this wasn't Niles as in Michigan. This was the Nile, like the Nile in Egypt. Why did his grandfather have an old map of Egypt out on the desk?

After another few minutes of flipping through the other pages, Horace covered the map and got ready to leave. Maybe there wasn't a secret door; just a pile of scraps his grandfather never threw out.

As he started walking out, he saw the antique grandfather clock against the wall. It had been damaged during the break-in. A small panel dangled from the side.

"Wait a minute," said Horace out loud, thinking of his dream.

His heart started beating faster. He scanned the clock, but there wasn't even the slightest indication of a keyhole. He then tried pulling at the sides of the old clock, but nothing budged. Finally he put his shoulder into the wood paneling and gave it a hard shove. It still wouldn't move.

Horace stepped back and bit down on his lower lip, deep in thought. The clock was the perfect cover for a secret door. It was the last place anyone would look.

He reached over and opened the glass door to the clock's face. He cradled the hour hand in one palm, the minute hand in the other. Horace could feel the weight of the steel pendulums as he wound the clock backward. Again and again he turned the hands, watching the heavy weights inside the glass rise like three steel balloons. When they reached their highest point, he waited for a sound, a chime—anything, really—wondering if the old antique would finally work and reveal a great secret. But nothing.

Horace closed the glass door and was getting ready to give up entirely, when he heard something. It didn't sound like the clock. It sounded more like a rattling of gears, coming from deep within the walls of the farmhouse. As if awoken from a long sleep, the grandfather clock suddenly swung open from the wall. There, where the antique time-piece had been, was a doorway.

He'd found it! The passage was hidden behind the clock.

Horace stepped toward the doorway and saw a spiral stone staircase that descended down into darkness. He let his toes dangle over the edge and took a deep breath.

This was a lot scarier than the basement. He gathered his courage and took a step. Then another, and another. The light from the office faded behind him, and he felt like he was entering an unknown world. His eyes grew in size at the thought of what treasures might await him.

And then a chilling sound filled the mysterious hole. The clock door slammed with a loud bang. He was locked inside the passage.

A terrible fear filled his veins. Would he die here? Who would even know to look for him? He hadn't told anyone where he was going.

Horace began to get dizzy. His breath came in short gasps as he ran through these possibilities in his mind, none of them hopeful. Not even a deep breath could ease the feeling that he was about to faint. In a final act of desperation, he reached into his pocket and remembered with disappointment that he'd left his phone in his back-pack. But then he noticed the beetle again. It didn't make sense. If the clock was the secret door, it didn't need a key. Then what was the beetle for?

As he pulled it out of his pocket, to his amazement, it began to glow in his hand. The beetle was alive. Its soft blue light illuminated the steps in front of him. Its effects were powerful, casting away not only the darkness of the tunnel, but also some of Horace's fears. Using the light from the beetle, he made a quick dash up the stairs only to confirm his dread. The clock door was locked shut. The only option was forward and into the darkness of the tunnel. He needed to get out of here alive.

After maybe a dozen more slow breaths, he resumed his descent. At the bottom of the steps he came out on a flat landing. *It must be a secret underground passageway*, he thought. Gradually, the passage tightened around him, sloping upward. Where was it all leading? He touched the ceiling with his hand to stop himself from bumping his head, and noticed a series of grooves on the cool surface. The light from the beetle was too dim to tell, but there seemed to be some type of markings on the walls.

He came to what appeared to be the end of the tunnel and a small set of wooden steps. Unlike everything else he'd encountered that afternoon, these looked relatively new. The steps brought Horace to a second door. He pressed with all his might, and the door flew open, bringing with it the smell of moldy grass. Horace recognized the room instantly and let out a huge sigh.

He wiped the dirt off his pants, then slowly stood up. He was in the shed at the back of the farm. It was just a hundred feet behind the house. This wasn't magical or special or even unknown.

Why did his grandfather have a secret passageway leading from his office out to the shed?

Horace pushed the shed door open and breathed deeply. The blue sky was a welcome sight after the darkness of the tunnel. He'd survived.

As he walked out into the field, trying to make sense

of his thoughts, he saw the unmistakable shape of Shadow circling above. The bird had never left. She dropped from the sky with a graceful arc and landed on one of the branches of the lone sycamore tree. The fall foliage of the tree was just starting to show hints of orange and red.

"I don't know, Shadow. None of it makes any sense."

The bird stood silent.

"Why would my grandfather have this tunnel? Maybe Sara and Lilly were right. Maybe it was a part of the Underground Railroad?"

Everything he had thought was wrong. The beetle wasn't a key—just a really cool flashlight. And the farm wasn't special.

"I guess it's time to head home."

He walked over to the tree to get Shadow's attention. She was totally preoccupied by a squirrel playing at the end of a branch.

"Shadow!" Horace shouted upward as he touched the tree for support. The trunk felt strong and weathered, firmly rooted in the ground. An old rope swing dangled from one of the lower limbs. His grandpa had been very protective of the tree, almost as much as he had been of the farm. Neither he nor his sisters had been allowed to play in its thick branches.

And then he saw it, just by chance, a small indent in the bark, no bigger than a thumbprint, at shoulder height.

Horace hesitated for a second and leaned in closer to be certain. Had someone tried to carve a name in it? No, it wasn't a name. He traced the outline with his fingers, and a rush of excitement passed through his body. Should he try? What was there to lose?

Slowly, he placed the beetle into the hole. The fit was uncanny. His memories of the next few moments felt like a dream. As he slipped the stone beetle into the smooth indent, the grooves in the tree's bark began to come to life. The small hole grew wider and wider, the bark moving like curtains opening onto a stage. Soon it was the size of a doorway.

The beetle was the key. And he'd discovered the door. Now only one question remained: Where did it lead?

chapter seven

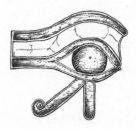

Without a moment's hesitation, Horace stepped through the magical door. Instantly he dropped into an endless ocean of spiraling blue and white shimmering waves of color that grew in intensity until nothing remained but a blinding light. It was like diving into the deep end of a pool, then being sucked through the drain, and then pulled into another pool, and another drain, and another pool. This went on for what seemed like hours, but what must have only been seconds, before Horace abruptly hit solid ground.

"Watch yourself, young man." Someone collided with Horace's arm, hard, knocking him back to reality. "This is a busy street."

Horace blinked, and the blue lights were gone. In their place was a blinding yellow sun, much stronger than any he had ever known.

"What?" A panicky feeling started to rise in his chest.

The man stared at Horace. "Do your parents know where you are?"

His parents? Horace didn't even know where he was. "Where am I?" he asked, confused. Somehow he was both understanding and speaking the man's strange language.

"This is Amarna, the City of the Sun. You must come from far away if you don't know that." The man gave him a piercing look. He tilted his head to the side, as if to say something more, then changed his mind.

Horace started scanning the landscape for anything familiar. What had happened to the farm, to the fields, to Shadow? The sounds and shapes were totally unknown. In front of Horace rose a sprawling metropolis of stone and sand, a secret city hidden deep within the roots of his grandparents' farmhouse tree.

He hadn't noticed it at first, but apparently when the landscape had changed, so had his clothes. He was wearing a small white robe with a golden threaded belt. On his feet were a pair of leather sandals, and a gold band was clasped around his wrist.

Yet the glowing blue beetle remained in his hand. He quickly slipped it into the pocket of his robe. He was about to ask the man another question, but when he looked up, the man had vanished.

This strange city was brimming with life as more and more people began to fill the streets. A small covered carriage pulled by two men passed, and Horace slipped behind it and into the safety of a nearby alley. He just needed a moment to collect his thoughts.

Horace bent down on his knees, hiding in the darkness of the alley, desperate to regain his senses. This place wasn't just foreign. It was old—really old. Almost like something out of his history textbook.

He began to run his fingertips through the sand. The small grains had a calming effect. He took another deep breath and traced several shapes. First he drew the farm, then the tree, the beetle, and then finally a question mark. So if the beetle was the key and the tree was the secret door, why here? And even more important, where was here?

Horace looked out at the busy street. If he was going to get any answers, he'd have to find them himself.

He ran his palm across the sand, brushed his hands together, and stepped out into the street.

Now he found himself in a swarm of men and women walking between the stone buildings. One woman was covered head to toe in a beaded dress. Each bead shimmered a different color, creating a rainbow of light that fell across her entire body. Even her long thick dark hair glistened with oil.

No sooner had the woman passed than another shoulder bumped his.

"Hurry up. You're late!"

To his surprise, it was a boy his own age.

The boy carried a clay tablet under his arm. "Come on. Let's go!" he shouted, and kept walking. Behind him, there was a group of more kids also dressed in white robes. This was probably his best chance to get some answers.

"Did you study your numbers tables?" Horace overheard one student ask another.

"Yes, I'm not taking any chances. Ay was so mad when I forgot last time."

"No kidding. Did you see how he yelled at us yesterday for not having our homework? You would have thought it was the end of the Epoch or something."

Apparently, it didn't matter where you were—homework always stunk.

The structures around the boys weren't just big and spacious; they were detailed and intricate. The walls were painted in beautiful hues of red and yellow. Against the sky, the tall, colorful columns resembled the tail feathers of a peacock. Even the capitals of the columns were decorated with floral motifs.

Horace felt something else pulsating around him, a strange energy that permeated the city. The sea of color, sound, and smell that surrounded him was only part of the magic. There was something special about this place, something different.

The group of boys continued to weave in and out of the streets, through the vendors, between the crowds, and into alleyways before finally emerging out into what appeared to be the heart of the city, a vast courtyard framed by two stone pillars.

Horace turned to the boy walking alongside him. "What is this?" he asked with growing courage.

"School, of course." The boy paused. "And the temple, too."

In the gleaming white light, the walls of a lofty rectangular structure stood out against the indigo sky. There were two tapering towers, each capped by a cornice and joined together by an entrance half their height.

As they passed inside, the smells were different: peppermint, lavender, and his favorite, cinnamon. The entryway was at least the size of half a football field, and it too was lined with pillars. In the center was an even more striking sight: the unmistakable towering statue of a man wearing a long cylinder-shaped crown and the beard of an Egyptian pharaoh.

It suddenly dawned on Horace. The beetle had opened a magical doorway to Ancient Egypt! He was in Egypt! Of all the places he'd imagined the secret door might lead, a connection to Ancient Egypt had been the farthest from his mind.

Horace racked his brains for what he knew about Egypt. He'd read about the pyramids, the Sphinx, the Nile, and even King Tut. But he'd never come across this place—Amarna.

It didn't make sense. Why here? What could be in Amarna?

But there was no time for his questions now. The boys around him kept walking toward the three doorways that led off the entryway, and Horace felt compelled to follow.

"Meet at the obelisks for lunch?" someone yelled.

"Sounds good!" a boy shouted back.

The group had started to split up, and Horace didn't know which way to go. He began to walk toward the left entrance. It looked as good as any, but before he could get very far, a firm hand stopped him.

"Hey, where are you going? The West Wing is only for the priests. You don't want to go in there." Horace turned to find another of the young boys next to him. He, too, wore a white robe. His head was shaved save for a single braid. "Class is this way." He pointed toward the hall on the right.

Horace hesitated. "Oh yeah, thanks." He tried to cover his mistake and quickly followed the boy through the right entrance.

It opened to an even longer corridor, this one lit by a series of torches. Many doors broke off from the main passage, some leading to rooms, others to even darker hallways. Halfway down the hall, the boy turned. Horace reached down and squeezed the beetle in his pocket. They had arrived.

The room they'd entered was an ancient classroom. Strangely, it had no chairs, no desks, and no books, just a giant carpet on an open floor. The teacher stood in the center. The boy in front of him walked to the side of the room and placed his stone tablet on a pile in the corner. The other students sat on their knees, reeds in their hands, already copying notes onto clay slabs. Most striking was the absence of any girls.

"Take a seat." The teacher stared intently at Horace, his eyes seeming to search for an answer to a question Horace didn't know. "You must be Horemheb's son. I thought you weren't coming for another week." He mumbled something under his breath before he continued. "We'll make do. My name is Ay." The name sounded like *hay*, just without the h.

Ay's white robe draped down to the floor. His smooth head glowed in the light; his hair was completely shaved. A single silver band clasped his wrist, and a thick gold ring circled his pinkie finger. His hands, soft and delicate, gripped one of the heavy stone slabs with ease.

"Where are your supplies?"

Horace struggled to gather his thoughts. If he were going to find any answers, he had to blend in. This might just be the opening he needed. "I . . . forgot them at home." Milton would have been able come up with something clever.

Ay shook his head in frustration. "You'll have to use mine, then. Here, take these." He handed Horace a dusty clay slab from the wall, as well as a wooden reed. "Tablets out, boys."

Horace glanced around the room. The other students started to copy the writing from a large stone tablet on the opposite wall. Horace had a small problem.

While the portal had transformed his clothes and allowed him to understand the spoken language, it hadn't given him any other skills he didn't already possess. And to make matters worse, the tablet was in hieroglyphics. But he couldn't blow his disguise. There was clearly some reason the door in the tree had led him to Egypt.

He sat there cross-legged and began to slowly copy each letter as best he could. To think he had complained so much about learning cursive!

Ay walked over and watched as Horace fumbled with the reed.

"You have terrible handwriting. Let's hope your incantations are better." Maybe Ay was Mr. Petrie's great-times-one-hundred-grandfather.

Horace bent over and began working with renewed fervor. Ay finally left his side and returned to the center of the rug. By the time Horace looked up again, he realized most of the other kids were already done, while he had only completed the first few lines. It was like trying to draw with a stick in the mud. Nothing was easy, and making curved lines was almost impossible.

Ay handed Horace a second tablet. "Let's see what you can do with this one."

Horace had no idea what it said or what to do. Ay would surely start to get suspicious at any second when Horace failed to decode this second tablet. In truth he was far less concerned about writing hieroglyphics and much more worried about what he was doing here.

"Do you need some help?" The whisper came from the boy to his right. It was the same one who directed Horace away from the West Wing.

Horace breathed a quiet sigh of relief. "Uhhhh, sure." He was hesitant to talk too much with anyone. The more he spoke, the more likely someone would figure out he didn't belong.

"Let's see." He took the tablet from Horace's hand and began to read.

"O', Atum. You became high on the height.
You rose up as the Benben Stone in the Temple of the Phoenix.
You set your arms about them as the arms of a Ka symbol
that your power might be in them."

Then the boy started to write. "How about this . . ."

O', Atum, you were high on the height.
You rose up as the Benben Stone in the Mansion of the
Phoenix.
You gave birth to the Ennead, you gave birth to the world,
and you set your arms about them as the arms of a loving
father, that your essence might be in them.

"That's great, but . . . but what does it all mean?" Horace's heart began to race.

The boy quickly carved a series of glyphs into his tablet. "It's complicated, but the most important thing is that it reveals the magic and wisdom of the Benben Stone. If Ay asks, just say it's part of the cycle of life and death. He loves that stuff." The boy smiled.

"So you've made a friend." Horace turned to see a mangled face staring over his shoulder. The man's nose looked like it had been broken multiple times, and his front brown-colored teeth were rotting. A black robe covered his deformed back, and his right eye seemed to twitch nervously as he spoke.

"Does he have a name?" the man asked the boy next to Horace.

Horace's face flushed. He was caught!

But before the boy could answer, Ay jumped in. "What are you doing here, Eke?"

Eke slowly lifted his gaze from the two boys and snarled. "I've come to get some of the tablets for the temple. The priests need them for . . . work."

Without turning around, Ay walked over, ignoring Horace, and grabbed the pile of clay tablets on the wall. "Now leave us alone."

"How generous of you, Ay. Sharing your precious supplies." Eke's voice dripped with sarcasm as he looked down over Horace's shoulder. "Teaching about the Benben Stone, are we? Don't confuse these boys with stories from the past." Eke lowered his head, revealing more of his rotting teeth. "The past is dead, Ay. You should know that. History has no place here in Amarna. Isn't that what our precious pharaoh used to say? But the future . . . Well, we'll just have to wait and see, won't we?" He smiled a terrible grin, then whispered down at Horace and the other boy, "Wait and see who is the next King . . ."

Eke said something more under his breath and then turned to leave, but his foot caught the bottom of his robe. The clay tablets went spilling out into the hallway, the boys laughing loudly at his misfortune.

Eke began to collect the tablets, when he stopped. "Laugh now, but we'll see who is laughing next time." Eke gave Ay a long sneer and then left.

Horace couldn't shake the goose bumps that lingered on his neck.

"Don't worry about him. He's all talk," Horace's new friend said reassuringly. "He's always like that, especially around Ay." The boy paused and made sure no one else was listening. "Those two never got along. He thinks Ay took his job."

"As the teacher?" asked Horace.

"No, he thinks he took his job as one of the head priests in the temple. Ay was one of my father's closest advisors, but now Eke's been trying to replace him. He's been running around spreading rumors about Ay and the other priests from Amarna. He says they're going to destroy the country and anger all the gods."

"What do you mean? Why would the gods be mad?" Horace whispered back.

"The same reason Eke and the priests are mad." The boy paused and scrunched his shoulders like it was obvious. "My father got rid of them."

First Amarna, then the Benben Stone, and now someone who had gotten rid of all the priests and the gods. How had those library books never mentioned any of this?

"Don't you know all that?" the boy asked.

Horace mumbled under his breath and then decided to change the subject. "What's your name?"

"Me?" The boy shot Horace a funny look, as if he should have known that, too. "I'm Tutankh, but all my friends call me Tut."

Horace's jaw dropped.

"Is something wrong?"

"Y-you're," Horace started to stammer. "You're King

Tut. The King Tut." He could hardly hide his surprise.

Tut only shook his head dismissively. "No, no, no. I'm not king. At least not yet."

chapter eight

"What's your name?"

"Me?" Horace hesitated then finally decided the truth couldn't hurt. "I'm Horace."

"Horace, like the god." Now Tut was the one who sounded surprised. "That's a pretty powerful name."

Horace had always thought his name sounded old-fashioned and boring, but Tut actually seemed impressed. He knew his name was connected to an Egyptian god, just spelled differently, and his grandpa had said it was also connected to the Dodge brothers, but those were the only two cool things about it.

A bell tolled deep within the walls of the temple, and

Horace half expected Mr. Witherspoon to announce a fire drill. Ay moved back to the center of the room. "All right, that's enough for one day. For homework, fill in the missing part of your tablets."

The other students nodded and started to pack up. This was Horace's cue to do the same, but he didn't know where to begin.

He needed to figure out a way home. Yet before he could slip out unnoticed, Ay pulled him aside.

"I don't know what you learned in Thebes, but we expect our students to have their supplies around here. Okay? Now don't forget your homework." Ay handed Horace another tablet covered in hieroglyphics.

Horace nodded anxiously. Ancient homework? What could be worse?

Tut came up next to him. "Do you want me to show you around?"

"That'd be great," Horace said with a mixture of eagerness and relief.

Ay interrupted, "As for you, Tut, you need to be back later this afternoon to practice. You have a lot to do and only a few weeks left."

"I know. I'll just show Horace some of the temple."

"That's fine—just stay out of the West Wing," Ay added firmly.

Suddenly the thought of going back to Niles didn't seem so important. Horace was about to be shown around Ancient Egypt and by none other than the famous King Tut!

Once they left the peaceful confines of the classroom, the halls of the temple brimmed with new energy and life. It seemed like everyone in the city had descended on the place. The light flickered across the faces of dozens of men and women who passed by as the two boys walked toward the entrance hall. Most wore the same long white robes as Ay, though a few sported robes of red, and even fewer, like Eke, dressed in black.

Horace looked over and saw a dark set of stairs leading down into another hallway.

"What's down there?"

Tut bent in even closer. "That's the West Wing. It's the most sacred area of the whole place and only open to the high priests. They say the priests keep the greatest objects of magic down there." His eyes opened even wider. "And they guard them with magical creatures. Ay use to tell me stories about wandering kids being eaten alive by the lions in the West Wing. I don't know if there's any truth to it, but I don't really want to find out."

"Neither do I." Horace felt a queasy feeling in his stomach. It sounded worse than the basement.

Two boys walked up to them through the crowd, breaking Horace's train of thought. "Hey, Tut," one said. "Are you free later?"

"Not today. I've got to practice with Ay."

"Lucky. We're on our way to the library. We've got to finish these scrolls." The boy held up a thickly rolled sheet of papyrus.

"That stinks. Maybe I'll see you around later," Tut answered politely.

"For sure." The boys smiled and disappeared into the crowded hall.

"What did you mean about practicing? What do you have to practice for?" Horace wondered if Tut had an important game coming up, or maybe even a presentation, like his own with Seth.

Tut eyed Horace suspiciously for a moment. "You don't know about my coronation? I thought everyone did. The coronation is the last ritual before becoming king."

Horace had read about Tut and his tomb, but he knew almost nothing about a coronation ceremony. In fact, most of the books he'd read barely mentioned Tut's life. Rather than risking saying something else stupid, Horace remained quiet.

The two boys kept walking until they entered an elaborately manicured courtyard full of towering palm trees, blooming flowers, and a bubbling stream that ran through the middle.

"Can I show you something? Promise you won't laugh at me or say anything?" asked Tut.

"Sure," said Horace, unsure of what might follow.

Tut sat down on one of the stone ledges outside the garden, then looked around to make sure no one else was watching. Slowly, he pulled up his robe, revealing the lower half of his left leg. It was contorted inward and looked like it was an inch shorter than his right.

Horace couldn't believe his eyes. King Tut had a club-foot.

Tut dropped his robe again. "See, I'm not made to be pharaoh."

Horace sat in stunned silence.

"That's why Eke keeps giving me such a hard time."

"Who'd be pharaoh, then?"

"I don't know. Probably my uncle Smenk. He's running the country now anyway." Tut looked sad. "It hasn't been easy since my father died. I used to know exactly what I was supposed to do, but now . . . I'm not even sure I should be king. My uncle and the old priests are still angry my father turned away from their gods. My uncle claims he cursed the country when he did it. And my leg . . . Well, I guess my leg is proof to them." Tut bent his head down. "I don't know. Maybe I wasn't meant to be a pharaoh. I can't run around like the other kids, let alone lead a kingdom. I would so much rather be like you. And just be normal."

"Trust me. It's not that great."

Tut grinned, but then shared more of his doubt. "At least the old pharaohs could claim they got their power from the Benben Stone, but now that's gone too. Not even the gods are on my side. I don't know what to do, Horace." Another moment passed in silence. "Sorry to be such a drag."

"No, I'm glad you told me. I promise not to say a word," Horace added, wondering more about the significance of this stone. It was the same one he'd read about on his tablet in class.

"Enough of this boring stuff. Let me show you my favorite place in the temple." Tut smiled. "I think you'll like it. Especially given your name."

Tut guided Horace through a bunch of other classrooms. In some, students were being taught math; in another room they were levitating objects; and in one class students were turning wooden staffs into snakes. Egypt was literally filled with magic!

Tut led Horace through a set of wooden doors as tall as the basketball hoops in the gym at school. Beyond was an enormous open space.

"It's a falconry!" said Tut.

Horace knew what a falconry was from his readings. It was common in the medieval world. Knights used the birds to hunt down small animals. They'd have elaborate competitions in the castles to see who had the swiftest and fastest bird. But he didn't know the Egyptians were one of the earliest civilizations to also train the animals.

"The first thing we have to do is find you a bird," added Tut.

Horace looked around and noticed a tree covered in colorful flying creatures.

Tut walked over and slipped a glove over Horace's left arm and then placed a small object that looked like an ancient whistle in his right palm. "You should probably try to start with one of the smaller birds. The big ones . . . Well, they can get a little snippy." Tut pointed to a tree near the opposite wall.

Horace walked toward the smaller tree, well aware from his experience with Shadow of how dangerous an angry bird could be. Slowly, he stuck his arm out toward one of the creatures. The bird closest to him let out a strange hiss and made a pecking motion at his hand. Suddenly the rest of the birds took flight at his approach, and the whole tree was empty.

Horace bit down on his lip in frustration. This wasn't going to be so easy.

He looked at Tut, who gave him another wave of encouragement, and Horace walked over to a second tree. Again, he lifted his arm—and nothing. This time the cast of birds didn't even move.

"Try again, Horace."

With Tut's encouragement, Horace sheepishly began to walk over to a much taller tree. This one filled with birds that looked to be the size of footballs. Horace couldn't help but notice their sharp talons, deadly claws squeezing tightly around the branches.

"Be careful. Those aren't as friendly," warned Tut. "Just walk calmly and confidently."

Horace swallowed and stepped beneath the towering canopy of this larger tree. He flinched as one of the bigger birds took flight and dove past his head.

"You're doing great!" Tut yelled from behind him.

Horace didn't think so. He was just hoping a bird didn't eat his ear for lunch. He slowly circled the tree, taking each step as quietly and deliberately as if he were trying to sneak into his sisters' room. While a few birds chirped at his presence, most seemed uninterested in his outstretched arm.

Finally, in one last attempt, Horace raised his gloved arm with great care and blew into the whistle. Barely a sound was made.

Horace took another deep inhale and tried again. This time the whistle gave a long and clear ring, echoing off the walls of the vast courtyard. Hundreds of birds—not just the ones in front of him—took flight. The sound was deafening. He wasn't even able to see Tut anymore through the shapes and sounds of the flying creatures. He feared he might have set off some unstoppable chain reaction.

Horace was ducking his head left and right, readying to run when, out of nowhere, he felt a firm grip snap on his gloved arm.

He blinked in shock. A single bird was perched firmly on the leather glove of his hand. It had worked! But this was only half the surprise. As he looked more closely, he noticed the bird was covered in speckled brown and black feathers, had two black eyes, and had a single yellow dot in the middle of its small forehead. Horace felt a chill run down his spine. He'd seen the bird before in Niles. It was Shadow.

"Great job, Horace!" Suddenly Tut was by his side.

The bird immediately leaped into the air.

Horace's face turned pale.

"Are you okay?" Tut asked.

Another bell tolled deep within the temple.

"Sorry, I think I just need to head home soon. I'm not feeling so well." What was Shadow doing here in Egypt?

Sensing a shift in his companion, Tut quickly changed the subject. "Don't worry. I'll show you back to the gate," Tut said reassuringly. "It's on the way to the palace. I saw you there by the obelisks this morning."

Horace nodded, realizing the obelisks must be the towering stone slabs he first saw at the gate. The same ones he'd seen in his dream. Maybe they were the other end of the secret door here in Egypt. Maybe they were his passage back to the future.

"Oh, thanks," said Horace with great relief.

"Just don't forget your homework." Tut smiled, handing Horace the tablet he'd been working on earlier in the day.

Horace took the tablet and then followed Tut out of the temple and into the city. As they walked through the streets, Horace found himself lost in a hundred new questions. Tut wasn't some stuffy pharaoh from his textbook, and he wasn't perfect, either. Tut's family seemed to have a lot of secrets, and perhaps the same thing might even be true of his own. Was Tut the boy who needed help? Help with what, though? But the falcon . . . Horace couldn't make any sense of how Shadow was in Ancient Egypt either. Could she have flown through the portal?

When the obelisks emerged above the walled city, Horace realized they'd reached their destination.

"I'll see you tomorrow, Horace?"

Horace smiled but didn't know how to answer.

"Just make sure you do your homework. Ay doesn't mess around."

"Thanks," Horace answered. "I'll be sure to finish it."

As Tut left Horace standing all alone at the edge of the city, a growing sense of dread and loneliness filled his heart. How was he ever going to get home?

He almost considered running after Tut, when he felt

something move in his pocket. The beetle!

It was still there. He looked around to make sure the streets were empty, then reached down and took it out.

The beetle came to life immediately in his hand, and this time two wings emerged from its back. Literally springing out of his hand, it hovered over his palm and then began to flutter toward the base of the towering obelisk on the right. Horace noticed another indent, just like the one he'd seen in the sycamore tree. He placed the beetle into the small indent.

A warm, blue doorway of light opened at the base of the granite pillar.

As Horace's eyes adjusted from the intense hues of blue that had just surrounded him, he realized he was back at the farm. In front of him was the shed; behind him, the sycamore tree. He stood still for a moment in the fields of the farm, gathering his thoughts. Traveling back in time to Ancient Egypt was beyond anything he'd ever imagined or dreamed.

He looked down and realized he not only had the beetle

in one hand, but he still held the clay tablet from class in the other. His sandals and robe were gone, though. He was back in his old clothes. Walking around the house, he also noticed his uncle's car. He quickly slipped the tablet into his backpack and started to jump on his bike.

A voice called from the front door. "Horace, what are you doing here?" Horace's uncle was walking toward him from the house. A second man stood on the porch. He wore an overcoat and a wide-brimmed hat, an odd outfit for a sunny fall day.

"I didn't see you out here earlier, but I found one of your tissues in the office." Horace's uncle held the tissue with his fingertips.

"I was just checking to see if my mom left her purse here."

His uncle looked unconvinced. "Listen, I don't want you snooping around. I have important business to take care of. Do you hear me?"

"Yeah," Horace said quietly.

"If I catch you here again, you're going to be in big trouble. Do I make myself clear?"

Horace nodded. "I understand."

"Now get home to your parents. It's getting late."

"What time is it?"

"It's almost six."

Horace ran the numbers in his head. He had spent almost an entire day in Egypt and only an hour or two had passed in Niles. The portal not only took him through space, it also altered time. Horace ran around the outside of the house and hopped on his bike.

As he began to pedal down the long dirt driveway toward town, a haunting shape circled overhead and let out a familiar high-pitched cry. Shadow was once again with him.

CHAPTER NINE

The next morning Horace awoke to a familiar knocking sound at his window. He ran over to the ledge to find Shadow flapping outside the glass pane. Beneath the windowsill was Herman.

Horace unlocked the two latches and lifted the window open. "Herman, what are you doing here?" Herman's hair was in disarray, and he looked like he hadn't slept all night.

"Horace, I need to know: Did you go through the portal yesterday?"

Horace stood there in silence. Was the portal the secret door at the farm?

"I have to know the truth. Did you go through the

portal?" he repeated.

Horace bit down on his lip. "Ummmm, maybe," he answered meekly.

"You mustn't go through the portal again. It's far too dangerous. The Order can't keep you safe there." Herman glanced quickly over his shoulder.

"What do you mean?"

"Please," he pleaded. "Stay in Niles and guard the beetle."

"But what about Tut? He might need our help. His uncle is trying to take the throne from him. And he doesn't have the Benben Stone to help him."

Herman's eyes narrowed. "What'd you just say?"

"Tut needs our help. His uncle and Eke don't think he should be pharaoh."

Herman shook his head. "No, what did you say after that?"

"The Benben Stone," Horace answered doubtfully.

"What do you know about the Benben Stone?" Herman asked.

Horace shrugged. "I don't know. The tablet I read

mentioned it was connected to the gods, and Tut said the old pharaohs had used it. But it's disappeared. No one can find it."

Herman suddenly looked incredibly agitated. "You have to trust me. You have to trust the Order. Don't go back through the portal. It is too dangerous."

"But what Order? You keep talking about this Order. Are there others who know about the beetle and the tree? Do they know about Tut and Smenk, too? Do they know about the Benben Stone?"

Herman's face turned expressionless. "I'm sorry, but I can't say any more right now." He paused before continuing in a stern voice. "Just do not go through the portal, and do not tell anyone—I mean anyone—about the beetle."

"Herman, why can't you just tell me what's going on?"

"What are you doing in there?" Horace's mom asked from the hall. "Are you talking to someone?"

Horace paused, surprised to hear her voice. "Ahhh, nothing, Mom. Just getting ready for school."

When he looked back out the window, both Herman and Shadow were gone. For a moment he'd been full of hope, possibility, and the excitement of traveling back to Egypt again. But now those feelings were replaced by a numbing frustration. Why wouldn't anyone tell him what was going on?

The rest of the week went by without incident. Horace kept the beetle close by his side but gave up on the idea of traveling through the tree again. At least his classes began to settle into a normal rhythm. Only twice did they get interrupted, but not by anything exciting or magical: once when Wally set fire to his notebook with a Bunsen burner, and a second time when Edith thought she'd spotted a mouse in the corner. More and more kids had begun to say hi to him, and Bryce had even asked if he'd wanted to play kickball. Milton was right: the stories about Horace's fight with Seth had definitely helped his reputation.

However, on Friday, when he sat down in Mr. Petrie's class and saw his peers nervously fumbling with their projects, a sinking feeling overcame him. It was the day of their class presentations on the ancient world. To make matters worse, Horace had done absolutely nothing with his partner since the fight. He and Seth were supposed to build a prop for the presentation, but they had never even met.

Anna and Milton were already at the front of the room. Mr. Petrie motioned for Anna to begin.

Anna cleared her throat. "The pyramids were believed to be ancient tombs for the pharaohs. People aren't really sure how the Egyptians built them. In some books we read, people said slaves built them. But others think"—she paused dramatically—"it was magic."

Milton ran to the other side of the room and hoisted a papier mâché block into the air with a fishing pole. The class laughed, and Anna continued. "But the real magic lay inside the pyramids. This was where the sarcophagi, or the dead bodies of the pharaohs, were found."

Milton stepped forward to unhinge two bolts on the side of a plywood pyramid. Together he and Anna pulled apart the giant wood structure to reveal a series of rooms and tunnels. A gasp went up from the class. Either they were amazed at Anna and Milton's ingenuity or frightened no one would ever top this presentation.

"Look inside," Milton said. It resembled a real pyramid. "This tunnel here"—Milton pointed to the entrance—"led to the tomb of the pharaoh." A small doll was wrapped in an aluminum foil crib. "And below it was another chamber for the queen and all her belongings."

"That looks like a dollhouse to me." Seth made his presence known from the back of the room.

"That's enough, Seth." Mr. Petrie stared at him with displeasure and then turned back to Milton and Anna. "Please continue."

"That's okay," Milton answered. "I actually used a lot of my sister's toys to make the inside." He didn't seem at all bothered by Seth's heckling. "The Egyptians believed they could take these things with them when they died." He motioned to the objects. In the two chambers, there were not just dolls, but also toy chairs, hats, clothes, and a candy bar.

"Can you believe all the stuff they put in these tombs? It's incredible!" Milton was beaming with excitement. "This was all part of the journey to the underworld."

The presentation went on to discuss the burial practices

and mythology connected to these great structures before Anna finally wrapped everything up. "And, hopefully, from our presentation, you can see why the pyramids are considered one of the Seven Wonders of the ancient world."

It was the best presentation Horace had ever seen, but that wasn't saying much. Last year at his old school one of his friends had dressed up like Davy Crockett to re-create a scene from the Alamo, which was cool until he crushed a computer keyboard after jumping over a desk to imitate the final charge.

"That was great!" Mr. Petrie said, clapping as Milton attempted to drag the pyramid over to the right side of the room. "Why don't you just leave your pyramid here for now? It will be a nice backdrop for the rest of the presentations." The backdrop was also a glaring reminder of what Horace and Seth hadn't done.

For the next hour Horace's classmates got up in front of the room, one pair after another, and spoke about their topics. From the Code of Hammurabi to the Lighthouse at Alexandria, Horace couldn't concentrate on any of it. He hadn't done a single thing to prepare for his own presentation. He hadn't even read a book. All week he couldn't stop thinking about Amarna. What was going on in Egypt? Why didn't Herman want him going back there? Was Tut in danger?

The sound of Mr. Petrie's voice broke Horace's concentration. "We have one final presentation before lunch. Our last group will be Seth and Horace." Mr. Petrie looked over at Horace.

Already in the front of the room, Seth had something in his hand. If Horace didn't know better, he'd say it looked like a roll of toilet paper. Horace reached down into his backpack, wondering if he might find something to use as part of his half of the presentation. Strangely enough, his hand hit a large object. He had totally forgotten about the tablet he'd brought from Egypt. He must have stuffed it into his backpack at the farm. He wasn't sure what he would do with it, but at least if Seth tried to attack him, he had a shield.

"Thank you, Mr. Petrie." Seth's voice was strong and clear. "We are excited to share our presentation on Ancient Egypt."

For a minute, Horace thought maybe Seth had prepared after all.

"Now for our presentation today, we decided to give a real-life demonstration of the mummification process."

"No, we didn't," whispered Horace under his breath.

"Yes, we did," Seth snarled.

"Is there a problem, boys?" This time it was Mr. Petrie who spoke.

"No," answered Seth firmly. "Take it, Horace."

Horace wasn't going to let Seth bully him anymore. He'd survived a trip to Ancient Egypt; he could handle Seth. "No."

"Do it!"

"What are you two trying to show us? Maybe you should just explain it," their teacher interjected.

"That's okay. We're just going to make Horace into a mummy." Some of Seth's friends started to laugh. "No one will miss him," he whispered in a sharp retort.

Horace's face reddened.

Seth started circling Horace's body with the roll of toilet paper.

"I said don't do that."

"Boys . . ." Mr. Petrie was starting to grow uneasy.

Seth tried again to wrap a second piece of toilet paper around Horace's waist. In the process, his hand grazed Horace's pocket and the beetle inside it.

"I said don't do that!" Horace knocked Seth's hand away with his left arm, and the roll went sailing across the front of the room.

Seth just stood there, stunned by Horace's brazen action. Mr. Petrie looked uncertain about how to handle the growing tension.

In an act of desperation and hoping to recover the presentation as best he could, Horace held up the Egyptian tablet still under his arm. "Ummm . . . Seth's not wrong; mummification was a very important part of the ancient world, and so was the process of the soul, or Ka, as the Egyptians called it, traveling to the underworld. In fact, the Egyptians took this journey so seriously, they carved in stone a detailed description of the journey to guide their loved ones."

Seth was now gathering up his toilet paper, probably so

he could use it against Horace later in the day.

"Continue," Mr. Petrie said.

Horace looked down at the stone in his hand. "This tablet is meant to represent one of those passages." Horace really had no idea what was on the tablet Ay had given him.

"That thing looks real," said Wally in the front row.

"What's written on it?" asked Mr. Petrie.

"Oh, these . . . umm . . ." Horace was starting to get that panicky feeling. "I just inscribed some hieroglyphics we saw in a book."

"Why don't you explain what it says to the class?" asked Mr. Petrie.

Horace stared at the script. He didn't know Egyptian.

"Go ahead," encouraged Mr. Petrie.

Horace began translating the hieroglyphics as best he could. "May my name be given to me in the Great House, and may I remember my name in the House of Fire." As he continued, things became easier. "I am with the divine one, and I sit on the eastern side of heaven. May my heart be with me in the House of Hearts! May my heart be with me in the House of Hearts!"

Horace let out a sigh of relief; maybe his travels through the portal had actually taught him something. But as he looked up again, he realized in his intense concentration he'd totally overlooked one thing: the entire class was now staring at him, their mouths open.

"Horace?" Mr. Petrie finally spoke. "When did you learn how to speak Ancient Egyptian?"

chapter ten

"That was incredible, Horace!" Milton said. "You totally showed Seth who's boss."

Horace shrugged.

"Seriously, look at him." Horace glanced across the lunchroom and saw Seth staring down angrily at his lunch.

"And you actually spoke Ancient Egyptian," Milton continued. "How cool was that?"

"Thanks," Horace answered humbly, and sat down with his two friends at their usual spot in the cafeteria. He was just relieved he'd narrowly avoided another disaster, as well as Mr. Petrie's prying questions.

"Yeah, that was quite the presentation," Anna added a

little more skeptically. "When did you learn all that?"

"I don't know. Over the weeks, I guess," answered Horace.

Milton continued, "Horace, tell us the truth. Did you buy that tablet on eBay?"

Horace took a deep breath. He still held the tablet from Amarna under his arm.

"It looks like it's three thousand years old," Milton said. "Better than even those letters I dipped in tea leaves last year. You must have spent a fortune on that thing."

"Or a hundred hours making it." Anna reached over and began running her hands over the coarse surface of the tablet. It smelled of dirt and clay.

Horace thought a moment about what Herman had said. He wasn't supposed to tell anyone. But Anna and Milton weren't just anyone; they were his friends. He could trust them, and, quite frankly, Herman had disappeared since his stern warning. Maybe he could just tell them a little. It felt weird keeping such a big secret. "Remember last week when I was late for school?"

"Not really," answered Anna.

"Horace, you're always late," added Milton.

"I guess that's true." He nodded. "But last week I was really late for homeroom. You see, I was getting ready to go to school, and this guy showed up. His name is Herman, and he delivered this mysterious package to me. Inside the package was a beetle." He looked around to make sure no one was near, and then placed the beetle on the table, next to the tablet.

"Wow," Anna whispered, staring at the symbol on the back.

"Yeah, this is pretty cool," added Milton with a smile. "Did you get a two-for-one deal?"

Horace laughed at Milton's remark then recounted to them how Herman also had the falcon called Shadow with him. And how he told Horace that Shadow would stay close to protect him.

"That's awesome," Milton chimed in. "I want a pet bird to protect me from Seth! I'd even use that bird on Ms. Shackles!"

Horace continued, "I think there is something going on in Niles though, maybe even connected to my grandfather's death. I overheard my parents talking about it last week." He bit down on his lip nervously. "I know, I know. It sounds totally crazy."

"Ummm, that might be an understatement," Anna answered.

His two friends were now staring at him like he'd lost his mind.

"I'm not making it up. Here, look." He handed Anna the beetle. "I read online that scarabs were used as seals for important documents or even charms. They were placed on the hearts of mummies to help with the passage to the afterlife. This beetle is some kind of symbol of rebirth. I think it has powers." Horace was hesitant to say any more.

Anna's eyes narrowed inquisitively. "Sorry, but tell me again. Where exactly did you find it?"

"I told you that."

"No, seriously, Horace. How did you get it? Milton's right. Did you buy it online?"

"I told you, this guy Herman delivered it in a package to my house." Less confidently, Horace admitted, "But I'm still not really sure why he gave it to me."

"And what about this tablet? Where'd you get that?" She reached over and touched it again.

Horace didn't know how to answer this, either. If they didn't believe the story about Herman, they definitely wouldn't believe a story about time travel. "I found it out at the farm"—he paused uncomfortably—"in the fields."

"Do you think it's real?" Milton asked Anna. "Or maybe it's, you know, like the relics."

"The what?"

"Horace, you must know about the Michigan Relics by now. Your grandpa made a big exhibit on them at the museum. He was the joke of the town for doing it."

"Hey, don't call my grandpa a joke." Horace looked angrily at his friend.

Milton could tell he'd touched on a tender subject. "Sorry, I didn't mean to say that," he explained. "It's just . . . the Michigan Relics, they were a bunch of artifacts found around here. Some people thought they were, like, five thousand years old. They had all these weird inscriptions on them that looked like ancient writing. But it turned out that the guys who found the stuff had made it all up. They ran a carbon dating test, and it all turned out to be only, like, a hundred years old."

Horace didn't know what the relics were or how his grandpa was connected to them, but he knew the beetle and the tablet were real. He'd traveled to Egypt and seen their power firsthand. He put the tablet in his backpack, and the beetle in his pocket. "Listen, I don't know what you're talking about, but these aren't fake, and they're not stolen." His emotions rose with every breath. "If you don't believe me, that's your choice. But I'm telling you the truth."

Anna sensed the change in Horace's tone. "Relax, Horace. Obviously, we believe you, but don't you think it's just a little suspicious?" She paused. "Did you ask your mom about it?"

Horace shook his head. "I didn't want to distract her. She's been busy trying to sort through stuff after my grandfather's death. And Herman insisted I shouldn't tell anyone. I'm not even supposed to tell the two of you."

"Don't worry. We won't say a word." Milton's tone had changed too. He crossed his heart with his hand. "But he didn't say you couldn't try to figure out where the beetle came from. A beetle from Ancient Egypt doesn't just magically show up on your doorstep. There's got to be something more to this. Let's go out to the farm to see if we can find out for ourselves."

"Ummm." Horace didn't know how to temper his friend's enthusiasm. "We could just read about it online first."

"Come on," Milton persisted. "Don't be so scared, Horace. How dangerous could it be?"

chapter eleven

As soon as they arrived at the farm, Horace realized he'd made a mistake giving in to Milton's excitement.

"This place looks like a mess." Anna gazed out at the backyard, almost immediately sensing the same danger as Horace. "Are you sure we should be here?"

"What do you think all this is for?" asked Milton. The grass was covered in spray paint and wood markers.

"I don't know, but it doesn't look good," answered Horace.

His uncle had padlocked the front door.

"So, let's search around. There's got to be more stuff out in those fields," Milton prodded.

"I don't know. Maybe we should just stay in the front." But it was too late. Milton had already run around the house and discovered the swing on the tree.

"How cool is this? Anna, give me a push."

"Milton, get off that!" Anna called.

Horace bit down on his lip and walked over to the shed. It was locked too. "My uncle's definitely up to something."

"What are we going to do now?" Anna said, noticing the lock.

Horace shook the handle in frustration.

"I really think we'd better get out of here," Anna added.

Horace was starting to think the same thing, when Milton pointed up toward the sky. "Hey, check it out. It's that falcon again."

Horace was surprised he hadn't noticed Shadow first. She was flying in a strange figure-eight pattern, something he'd never seen her do before.

"She looks really nervous," Anna said.

"Yeah," answered Horace, wondering what could be up.

"Maybe it's some kind of warning," said Milton.

But why would she be giving us a warning? Who would she be warning us about? thought Horace.

The answer to his question came in the sound of tires pulling up the gravel driveway.

He recognized the black sports car instantly. "Oh no . . ."

"Who is it?" asked Anna, sensing Horace's change in tone.

"My uncle."

"Why's that bad? We'll just tell him we were looking around," said Milton nonchalantly. "Your family owns the house. It's not like we're trespassing."

Sweat was starting to form on Horace's brow. "No, you don't understand. I'm not supposed to be out here." He quickly scanned the field. "If he catches me again, I'm going to be in big trouble." There was no place to hide in the open field, and the car was now more than halfway up the long driveway.

"What should we do, then?" asked Milton.

Horace desperately searched around for some kind of cover. And then he had an idea.

It was risky, but it might be their only chance. They'd

just hide there for a few minutes and then come right back, he told himself. His uncle would be gone, and no one would be the wiser.

He could see Shadow now flying in tighter circles.

"Milton, grab my hand. Anna, grab Milton's. I'm not exactly sure how this works, but I think we need to hold hands as we go through it."

"What do you mean? Go through what? What are you doing, Horace?" asked Milton.

"Just trust me."

Milton finally jumped off the swing and grasped Anna's hand. The sound of a car door opening could be heard on the other side of the house.

"Ready?"

"Are we going to start running around the tree, chanting?" asked Milton halfheartedly. "I'm not sure this will impress your uncle."

"No, but close." Horace took the beetle out with his free hand and placed it in the indent on the tree. The door of light opened, and in the next moment the three of them passed through the portal.

Anna was in shock, her jaw agape.

Milton's eyes were two giant saucers staring at the gold bands on his wrist.

"Are you guys okay?" Horace asked with growing concern. Neither had made a sound since their arrival.

Milton was the first to break the silence. "I can't believe it. Check out this robe. This is so cool! Is this some kind of dream?"

"Or a nightmare," added Anna. "Where are we?"

"Egypt," answered Horace. "We're in Ancient Egypt. Well, Amarna, to be more exact. I was trying to tell you guys about this at lunch. The beetle opens a secret door at the farm that links back to the past."

"Like time travel?" asked Milton.

"Exactly," answered Horace.

"You guys," Anna muttered with great hesitation, "we need to get out of here."

"No way!" answered Milton. "We just got here. Let's explore a little."

Horace tried to reassure her. "I've been here before, Anna. I can show you around. We'll only stay a few minutes, and then we'll go back through the portal to the farm. By then my uncle will be gone."

"I *really* think we need to be getting out of here, guys."

"Anna, you are always such a worrier. Let's trust Horace. How dangerous could this place be?" protested Milton.

"Ummm . . ." Anna pointed over Horace's head.

A horde of people was charging toward them. One small older man was running in front yelling, "Smenk's army! They're coming to destroy the last remnants of Akhenaten's priests!" A trumpet sounded, and a thick cloud of smoke appeared in the distance.

"Don't stand there! They're coming!" a balding man with a scruffy beard yelled frantically as he hurried by the three of them. Two more women in long hooded gowns were right behind him, ushering a group of little kids through the gates.

Horace looked back at the base of the obelisk, only to realize their chances of getting through the portal were gone. The base had turned to stone, and the number of people running through the street made it all but impossible to escape unnoticed. To make matters worse, in the distance, a mass of dust hovered over the dunes. From within its midst, rows of men, horses, and chariots charged toward them.

"Hurry up!" a woman yelled. "They're closing the gates!"

Citizens in beige robes, drenched with sweat and covered in dirt, pulled a giant metal chain from one of the ramparts.

"What should we do?" Milton asked Horace.

They had two options: stay and potentially get killed by the attacking army or run into the city and find safety. Horace made up his mind. "We have to get to the temple."

"Temple?" asked Milton.

"Just trust me. If we are going to get out of here alive, we are going to have to get into the temple. There is someone there who might be able to help us."

Horace's friends didn't need any more prompting. They ran quickly behind him, joining the last group of distraught citizens slipping into the walled city.

Inside the city gates, carts of food had been turned on end, and homes had been boarded up. Men charged toward the walls, carrying improvised weapons. Some of these sudden warriors looked like they'd just left their trades, and wielded what appeared to be spears. Others carried strung bows. Even the statues, which once stood as strong, stoic guardians, shook from the vibrations of the distant army.

Horace led them toward what he thought was the heart of Amarna. They weaved through wreckage, scaling makeshift barricades and dodging the groups of men running to meet Smenk's army at the gate.

A dark-skinned teenage boy, eyes terrified, came at them. "Run! Run!" he repeated, motioning in the opposite direction. "They're coming for us!"

Horace ignored the warning and continued to plow forward.

They passed through a walled courtyard and another alley, where they found only weeds and broken wicker baskets. Undeterred by the dead end, Horace doubled back, looking for a new route. After two more wrong turns, he finally found the passage of stone sphinxes that led to the temple.

Two guards stood with shields and swords behind the iron bars of the temple gate, their hair blowing from the forceful gusts of wind.

"Excuse me," Horace said. The men looked down at him and he braced his body, projecting infinitely more courage than he actually felt. "I need to get inside."

The man on the right spoke in harsh tones. "No one is allowed to enter the temple. By orders of the priests."

"My friend is in there." Or so Horace hoped.

"No one," the guard repeated.

Horace walked into the open square. He was desperate now. If they didn't find Tut, they would certainly be killed in the assault on the city. But at the same time, Horace didn't know where to hide. The sound of a deep drumming was growing louder. The invading army was right at the edge of the city gates.

There had to be another way inside, Horace told himself. Or at least a place to hide.

"Are you sure you know where you're going?" Milton asked Horace.

He shook his head doubtfully. "No, but we really don't

have a lot of options." The sounds of explosions were growing louder and louder. The invading army would overrun the city at any moment.

Horace led Milton and Anna toward an arched alleyway that ran out of the square. If he couldn't find a way in, he had to at least find them some better cover. But the doors and windows lining this street were already boarded up. From the layers of soot that had gathered along the shutters, they looked like they'd been closed for weeks.

"Whoever lived here sure left in a hurry," said Anna.

They walked farther down the street, where the high walls of the alley started to block out almost all the light. The street took a hard right and then a left, and from what Horace could tell, seemed to be winding its way around the temple. After the sixth abrupt turn, he had begun to question bringing them into the city at all.

The heavy clouds of smoke that passed overhead had blocked all the remaining light. The distant sound of shouting had combined with the roar of large explosions in rapid succession. The soldiers must have already broken through the gates.

"What should we do?" Milton yelled over the din.

It was Anna who had the answer this time. "Down there." She pointed across the street to a doorway.

The dark had obscured a small gap at the base. It was small, the size of a hole a possum might burrow into the side of a tree, but it was wide enough for them to slide through.

The sounds of threatening voices grew louder. There was no time to waste. "I'll go first and make sure it's safe." Horace bent down on his knees and pushed his way past the loose boards. He could feel the splintered wood scraping against his skin. He winced in pain. He just hoped this wasn't another dead end or worse, a death trap.

To his relief, the boarded-up house was empty.

Once inside, Anna and Milton gasped as their eyes adjusted to the faint light. "Whoa." Scrolls stacked high against the far wall, clay tablets were piled next to a fireplace, and a large wooden table laden with more tarnished, old scrolls stood in the center of the room. On the floor, next to a worn rug, was another pile of papyrus.

Milton sifted through the shelves and tablets. "Look

at all this stuff. These look like my posters from last year's science fair." Milton opened a roll of Egyptian papyrus with strange geometric shapes etched along its surface.

Anna held open another scroll, this one covered in hieroglyphics. "It looks like someone was trying to decode an ancient formula."

Horace picked up a sheet of papyrus with a small red wax seal on the corner.

But his exploration was cut short by the sound of heavy footsteps and clanging armor in the street.

Horace ran over to the door and laid a scrap of wood across the hole they'd just climbed through. Just as he was starting to think about their next move, a second, much quieter sound filled the room, almost like an eggshell cracking.

"What was that?" asked Milton in a whisper.

All three of them froze.

The sound came again, slightly louder.

"I think it's coming from over there," Anna whispered as she pointed to a fireplace in the wall.

Milton grabbed a scroll, holding it like a weapon,

while Horace reached down, readying to remove the wood by the door and escape back out into the street. Then, suddenly, the cracking turned into a loud rumble, and the entire stone wall of the fireplace thrust open.

There, in the dim light of the fireplace, stood the silhouette of a girl.

chapter twelve

The girl stepped forward, and Horace was struck by her long black hair and golden headband. While she looked tired, and her clothes were covered in dirt, her eyes were radiant. Around her neck hung a golden necklace in the shape of a cross, with a circular top. The metal seemed to shimmer from a magical light that lit up the dark room.

She was just a kid. And by the looks of it, the same age as they were.

Horace regained his bearings and tried to put her at ease. "Don't worry. We're not here to hurt you." He gestured toward his friends. "This is Milton, and that's Anna. And I'm Horace."

The girl's eyes opened wide. "Horace?" she said, peering more closely at him.

"Do you know her?" Milton asked.

Horace shook his head subtly. He had never seen this girl before, but he didn't want to be rude.

"Tut mentioned you," she explained as she wiped a flake of dirt from her face with her fingertip. "I'm Meri."

It was difficult to know who was more surprised, Horace or Meri.

"You know Tut? King Tut?" Milton almost shouted.

"Shhhhhh," encouraged Horace. "There are still guards out there."

The girl didn't seem to mind, though. "Yes, I'm his wife." She paused, noticing the look of even greater surprise on their faces. "His future wife, once he becomes pharaoh. Our parents arranged our marriage. It's common among royalty."

"Is Tut okay?" asked Horace. "I thought he might be in trouble."

"Smenk and his army have come for him and the priests. Many people think Smenk has the blessing of the old priests, since he also claims to have possession of the sacred Benben Stone."

"What's the Benben Stone?" asked Anna.

"It's the magical stone from the Old Kingdom," Meri answered.

"And now Tut's uncle has it?" asked Horace.

Meri walked over to the door and peered into the small hole they'd crawled through, checking to make sure no one was in the alley. "I don't know anymore. Everything has changed since Akhenaten's death."

"That's Tut's dad," Horace told his two friends. "He was the one who created this city."

Meri continued, "When Akhenaten built Amarna, he also closed all the temples along the Nile that were connected to the earlier gods. Many of the priests were angry they'd lost their jobs."

"But what does any of this have to do with the Benben Stone?" inquired Anna.

"Some, like Smenk, believe if they find the lost Benben Stone, they can reawaken the power of the old gods and destroy this city and Aten, the sun god, with it.

The ancient temples along the Nile would be reopened, and everything would go back to the way it used to be."

"You mean, with the priests in charge again," Anna added.

"Right." Meri nodded.

"But I don't see what's so bad about the priests being in charge?" pressed Milton.

"Before," Meri answered, "if you had a problem, you had to ask the priests for help, and only if they felt you were worthy enough did they petition the gods on your behalf. Here in Amarna, Akhenaten made the sun god, Aten, available to everyone. The priests no longer controlled our connection to the gods. The power was in the hands of the people."

"So let me get this straight," Milton said. "If Smenk has this Benben Stone, he will destroy this city and try to destroy any signs of Akhenaten and his new god, Aten, so he and the former priests will be in charge again? But if we stop him, we might be able to preserve the idea of Amarna?"

Meri smiled. "Yes."

"How are *we* going to do that, though?" asked Milton. "It seems like a lot for four kids."

"By helping Tut," said Horace. "If he becomes pharaoh, he can preserve the memory of his father and Aten."

"And by stopping Smenk from getting the Benben Stone," insisted Meri.

"But I thought you were trying to help us figure out a way home, Horace," accused Anna.

Before Horace could answer, the sound of footsteps and shouting in the alley made the kids duck.

Meri waved her hands and mouthed, *We must get you out of here.*

"But where?" Horace whispered. "The whole city is under attack."

Meri stood still for a second as she muddled something over in her mind. Then she walked over to and reached into the fireplace, digging through the ashy logs with her hand and then finally pulling down a hidden lever. A second wall opened. "Follow me."

As if reading their minds, Meri turned her head. "When I was younger, I'd sometimes sneak out of school with my sisters. We discovered every secret hiding spot in the temple, and every way in and out."

Anna smiled. "I wish we had one of these. I'd use it to get out of gym."

Meri looked a little confused but continued, "We can use this tunnel to slip into the temple. There we can look for Tut and then escape out through the cisterns."

"Huh? The sisters?" asked Milton.

"The *cisterns*, underground tunnels that supply water to the city. Once we find those passageways, we can follow them out of the temple. They'll lead us to the edge of Amarna. We can get to them through the West Wing. Almost all the stairwells to the catacombs and crypt lead there."

Horace swallowed at the thought of going down into an Ancient Egyptian basement.

"This door will close soon," she warned. "And we don't want those guards to find us here."

Horace, Milton, and Anna didn't need more encouragement. All three stepped into the dark passage together.

As soon as Meri entered, the hidden door closed

behind them. Once again, they found themselves in near darkness. The slivers of light from several cracks in the ceiling illuminated the long corridor. From what they could see, the tunnel appeared to have been cut through the limestone walls of the temple. Spider webs framed the dark corners, and the only sign of life was a small mouse that scurried past their feet.

As the four of them moved forward, Horace began to wonder how safe the inside of the temple might really be. It would only be a matter of time before Smenk's army descended upon it.

Finally they came to the end of the tunnel, where they met a solid stone wall with a rusting bronze knob in the shape of a lion's head. Meri reached out and pulled on the handle, and a giant slab of stone slid to the side. The second door opened, releasing a wave of hot air.

The sacred halls of the temple opened before them.

chapter thirteen

No sooner had their eyes adjusted to the light of the temple's interior halls than the flickering of moving torches danced across their faces. "Quick! Someone's coming." Meri pointed toward a wooden door. The four of them, desperate for cover, dashed across the hallway and disappeared from view.

Another minute passed as they huddled in the dark closet, and a wave of footsteps rushed by. Horace was about to step back into the hall, when a pair of feet paused outside the door.

With the help of the torchlight from the hallway, the four of them looked around and saw what appeared to be shelves on one side and giant jars along the other. Horace pointed at the jars. He and the others scurried out of the way and hid behind two particularly large clay vessels. The door opened and light filled the room, exposing their old hiding spot.

As a man peered cautiously around the door, Horace could see his twisted nose and deformed spine against the light of the hall. It was Eke, Smenk's closest henchman. Eke peered down at the three big jars and sniffed. For another few seconds he searched the musty space. Then, convinced no one was there, he finally closed the door again. Horace let out a long exhale.

The four kids waited another moment and then popped out into the dark corridor. The shadow of Eke's disfigured body shuffled down the hall.

"Who was that guy?" Milton asked. "He smelled terrible."

"You don't want to know." Horace shook his head, remembering his encounter with Eke in the classroom.

Meri looked around the door's edge. "We need to stay away from him. He's up to no good. Let's try this way." She pointed in the opposite direction.

Everyone quietly tiptoed down the hall. They caught a last glance of Eke as he took a left turn at the end of the corridor.

By the time they reached another hall, they thought they'd escaped danger and lost him for good. The walls of the temple had completely changed from limestone to black marble, and Horace knew where they were.

"This must be the West Wing," he said. "But where do you think Tut is?"

Meri had no answer. There was no sign of anyone, and even she seemed lost. When they turned to retrace their path, suddenly the sound of approaching footsteps echoed through the stone halls, and again the four of them dashed for cover.

This time, however, the door they'd slipped into didn't lead to a storage closet, but to a giant rectangular room lined with torches. A raised granite platform rested in the center. Horace wondered if it were one of the ceremonial rooms used by the priests.

They heard approaching voices and Meri quickly led

them behind a column near the door.

In a matter of moments two men entered the room. Horace immediately recognized Eke, but he didn't know the lanky second figure. He was even more sinister-looking than Eke and at least a head taller. They seemed to be debating something. Horace's heart started to race.

Four more men marched in, each holding the ends of two long poles. In the center was a golden platform holding a black, speckled stone covered in ancient symbols. It was about the size of a pumpkin and shaped like a pyramid. The black stone shimmered a purple hue from beneath its granite surface.

"Be careful with it," the man next to Eke commanded in a shrill voice. "Steady, steady. We must make sure it is in perfect condition."

With great care, the men lowered the apparatus onto the altar in the middle of the room. From their effort, it appeared that this small stone was heavy—incredibly heavy—for its size. As soon as the stone touched the altar, the men slowly removed the two long poles and stepped back toward the doorway.

"What about the priests?" Eke asked.

"Bring them in," the tall man answered.

There was a shuffle of movement, and four more men entered. The two with swords hanging from their belts were clearly guards. The other two were shackled prisoners. Horace recognized their shaved heads and white robes. They were priests from the temple.

The tall man ignored the two prisoners and began circling the stone like a vulture over a field. Horace could hear him whispering under his breath, but he couldn't quite make out what it was—perhaps some ancient spell or sorcery. Finally the man stopped, and he reached his fingers out to touch the intricate symbols. As he rubbed the stone's dark surface for the first time, it pulsed a deep purple. Then it went still. He ran his fingers frantically over its fine etchings, but nothing happened—no color, no sound, not even a spark of light this time.

His face contorted into a mixture of frustration and anger.

Horace felt like a pail of cold water had been poured down his whole spine. There was something deeply unsettling about the man's hollow eyes and bony fingers.

"There is a way. I can see it on your faces." The man's voice crackled with rage as he stepped away from the altar. He pointed to the priest on the right, and Horace's eyes widened. It was Ay. "You! Fix it."

But Ay stood still, courageously, without flinching or making a sound.

A red bolt leaped from the man's staff and struck Ay in his chest. He fell, writhing on the ground. The man spun and pointed his staff at the second priest. "If you do not speak, I will kill him."

The priest sighed in defeat. "I will tell you."

A horrible smile came across the tall man's face. "These priests have little tolerance for pain," he whispered to Eke.

He motioned for the second priest to continue, but when the terrified man hesitated, another bolt of light struck the ground inches from Ay's face. "Don't waste my time!"

"It can't work, Smenk. It will not work without the key," the priest cried.

Horace felt his stomach drop. The evil man was

Smenk, Tut's uncle.

"Key? What key?" Smenk scoffed. "There is no such thing." He sent another bolt of red light directly to Ay's chest. Ay screamed.

"I'm telling the truth," the other priest begged.

Smenk narrowed his eyes. "Then what is it? An *ankh*, an amulet, a word, a name? A sacred spell? What is the key to the Benben Stone?"

The priest shook his head. "A scarab beetle."

chapter fourteen

The weight of Ay's words dropped in Horace's stomach like a rock. Was his beetle also the key to the Benben Stone? He looked down and noticed the scarab was glowing in his pocket.

A muffled sneeze caught his attention. Milton had his arm across his mouth, making a choking sound and trying desperately to hold back a second sneeze.

"What was that?" Smenk pointed his torch in the direction of the column.

They had been spotted. Horace stood there for half a second longer before finding his voice. "Run!"

All four of them bolted out of their hiding spots at

the same time. They shot past the guard at the door, easily dodging his slow reaction, and darted into the hall.

"Get them!" Smenk commanded.

But Horace and his friends were already sprinting down the marble corridor. Horace couldn't see well in the darkness and narrowly avoided a fatal collision with a wall when he took a hard right turn. He could hear the soldiers behind them getting closer.

Out of nowhere, Horace felt the floor drop from below him and realized he'd found the steps. Fortunately, it wasn't a big drop. He rolled across the floor as he hit the hard ground. Milton, more aware of his surroundings, jumped down the steps two at a time. A wave of relief swept over Horace as Milton, too, made it safely to the underground passage. But then he saw Anna, still at the top, tangled in her robe. Meri was with her, trying to help.

"Hurry, Anna!" he cried.

But as he called out her name, Eke appeared at the top of the steps with two more soldiers and grabbed both girls by the arms.

Horace and Milton stood at the base of the stairs,

staring up in dismay. "Anna! Meri!"

Anna looked down at Horace. "Get out of here. Don't let them catch you."

But he couldn't leave Anna and Meri behind. And where was Tut? They'd all be killed!

He felt a pull on his sleeve. "Horace," Milton urged. "We've got to get out of here or we'll never be able to help them."

Horace looked up as several more guards came running toward them. At the same time, Horace could see Eke starting to tie Anna's wrists with rope, and another guard was holding Meri by her robe.

Milton was adamant. "I don't want to leave her either, but if we want to be able to help, we've got to leave now!"

Horace caught Anna's eye.

"Go!" she yelled down the stairs.

"What do we have here?" Smenk's voice had an unmistakable crackling sound to it. "The temple is always full of little treats." He pointed down at Milton and Horace. "Now grab them."

That was all the encouragement either boy needed.

Horace darted down the long underground hall with Milton in the lead. When he finally caught up to him, it was just in time to hear Milton yell, "Jump!"

Horace expected to land on another staircase. Instead came a current of cold water. His head popped back up above the water's surface, and he gasped for air.

"Well, I think we found the tunnels out of here," said Milton, his head bobbing just a few feet in front of Horace. Despite everything, he still held on to his sense of humor.

"We can follow them out to the city gates," answered Horace, remembering what Meri had told them.

They were being carried by the water at top speed as the tunnel twisted and turned its way through a maze of underground passageways, the walls changing color from seaweed green to a dim yellow. The shadows of their pursuers receded into the distance.

It looked like they might have finally escaped, until Horace heard another problem.

"What's that sound?" he shouted to Milton.

The two of them could see a light in the distance and hear the growing roar of water—a waterfall.

"Swim to the left side!" shouted Horace. "There's a ladder carved into the wall of the tunnel up ahead."

Horace could see the outline of a ladder getting closer. He began to maneuver his body as Milton did the same in front of him. "Grab the ladder and don't let go!" yelled Horace. The waterfall was approaching rapidly. He wasn't sure how he was going to do it, but it didn't look like he had much time. He saw Milton grab the bottom rung of the ladder. Horace closed his eyes as he reached up. He held on tightly to something.

As he opened his eyes, he realized he hadn't grabbed the ladder, but Milton's arm. Horace looked across his right shoulder and found they were only feet away from being thrown over a huge drop. The thunder of the water was now almost deafening.

"Hurry!" Milton yelled. "Pull yourself up." Horace could see him struggling to hold on to the slippery stone.

Horace turned back, tensed his muscles, and gritted his teeth. He began to pull himself up off his friend's arm and onto the ladder.

"Keep going!" Milton urged.

And then he was fully on the ladder. He looked down, and Milton was starting to pull himself up too. Horace turned around and began to climb. It was only about eight rungs high, not much taller than the ladder on the school playground, but the rushing water below made it infinitely scarier. When he reached the top rung, his fingers grazed a grate. Horace reached out with his right hand and, to his relief, it easily popped open. He pulled himself onto the dirt street above. He blinked in the midday light, a sight he hadn't been sure they'd ever see again. In the distance stood the obelisk at the city gates.

Milton was right behind him, panting, his robes dripping with water.

Horace could feel his tears mixing with the moisture from the cisterns, partially from relief, but also from despair. Anna was now in the clutches of Smenk, and Horace could hardly bear the thought of what he might do to her.

And his beetle wasn't just a key to the portal. It was the key to the Benben Stone. He knew it in his bones. That was why Herman didn't want him going through the portal. Horace had unknowingly almost delivered the beetle right into Smenk's hands.

The two boys walked over to the obelisk, and Horace turned toward Milton. "Listen, time goes by really fast here. When we get back to Michigan, we have to find a way to return soon. A couple of hours in Niles is days in Amarna."

"What are we going to tell our parents, then?"

Horace was now deep in thought. "We'll tell them we were working on a homework assignment and we need to meet up to finish it."

"But what if they start asking about Anna?"

Horace swallowed. "We'll just tell them she went to the library."

"Horace, the library closes at five. No one is going to believe that."

He was struggling to come up with a better idea, but luckily Milton had one.

"I've got it. You tell them she went to my house, and I'll say she's at your house. By the time they figure out she's not at either house, hopefully, we'll be back here."

"Good idea."

"But one more thing, Horace."

"What is it?"

"How are we going to rescue her from Smenk?"

Horace bit down on his lip. "I don't know."

chapter fifteen

Horace walked into the kitchen of his house and dropped his backpack onto the floor. He tried to wipe the sand from his arms and with it, any suspicion of what had happened. Unfortunately, it wasn't more than a matter of moments before his mom began to pry.

"So, where were you this afternoon?"

"Oh, just finishing homework with Milton and Anna."

"Was that it?"

"Well, we went for a bike ride," Horace answered, hoping this was all she'd ask.

"Is there something else you want to tell me?" his mom dug.

Did she know about Anna?

"Your uncle told me he saw your and your friends' bikes out at the farm. I thought we talked about this."

Horace hesitated. One part of him desperately wanted to tell his mom all that had happened, but he also knew she wouldn't understand and it would only make Anna's situation worse.

"Horace?"

"I . . . I guess we rode out there. We just walked around. I wanted to show them the fields in the back." It wasn't completely untrue.

"Did you go inside the house?"

"No," Horace answered sheepishly.

"Horace?"

"I promise we didn't. It was locked."

"Listen, your uncle is doing some renovations, and it's not safe for you to be walking around there. You understand?"

"Yes," he answered quietly.

She continued, "Now, Anna's parents called. They said she hasn't come home for dinner. Do you know anything about that?"

He cringed. He had to play it cool. "Yeah, after the farm we went over to Milton's. I think she's still there."

"Oh, okay. I'll just call her mom and let her know."

"No!" Horace realized his response was a little too forceful. "I mean, I'll just text Milton. You don't have to call. I'm sure they're finished with their homework by now."

"Horace"—she walked over and gripped him in a warm hug—"I know it's been tough since Grandpa died. We're all trying our best. It takes time. But if something is wrong, you've got to let me know. Okay?" She seemed to be hinting at something more but wasn't saying it.

Horace buried his head into her sweater, hoping to squeeze out all that had happened that afternoon. If only she knew the half of it.

For the next hour as he sat at the kitchen table Horace pretended to be busy with his math homework, while in the margins he listed out every possible scenario of what might happen to Anna if they didn't rescue her soon. First, Anna could die. Smenk clearly had no problem killing people. Second, Anna and Tut could both die! Although Horace still wasn't certain where Tut was. And third, all of them could die, Anna, Tut, Ay, and Meri! He quickly crumpled up the paper and threw it into the trash. It wasn't helping.

Finally his dad's car could be heard in the driveway. When he walked into the house with Horace's sisters, all three immediately sensed something was up.

"What happened to you? Did one of your fish die?" asked Lilly as she poured water into his glass at dinner.

"Just leave me alone." Horace's hair was a mess, and he'd been chewing on his pencil so hard, it was down to a nub.

"Fine, but you really shouldn't mope around like that. You look like the Hunchback of Notre Dame."

Horace grabbed his glass and took a big gulp of water. He hadn't realized how thirsty he was after the trip through the portal.

Sara reached out and squeezed his shoulder. "Don't worry, Horace. It'll get better. I promise. We all have bad days."

Horace looked up, confused. Was this his same sister? The one who had threatened to sell all his toys at a yard sale? Sometimes he forgot Sara had once been his age too.

"Thanks," he answered meekly. He really hoped more than anything things would get better soon. He just wasn't sure how.

Another few minutes passed as their mom finished serving dinner. His dad went around, asking them each how their day was. Then halfway through dinner, it became clear their dad also had something else on his mind.

"I want to talk to you guys." His voice sounded earnest, never a good sign.

"What is it?" Lilly asked. "Are we moving *again?*"

"No. We're not moving," he answered, trying to calm the fears from their last serious family conversation. "It's about Grandma and Grandpa's house."

"The farm?" Horace asked.

"Yes, the farm," his dad continued. "Your mom and I have been talking with your uncle. Apparently, the farm is prime real estate in Cass County. And . . . we've decided to sell it."

"What?" Horace gasped. "You can't sell the farm! Grandpa would never want us to sell it! And what about Grandma? When are we going to go see her?"

"Now calm down, Horace," his mom replied. "Your grandma is not well. She needs time to adjust to her new home. And we need the money to pay for the nursing home as well."

So his grandma was at a nursing home. That was why she hadn't been at the farm. And the strange man with his uncle at the farm, he must have been a prospective buyer. If they sold the farm, he might never get a chance to go through the portal again.

Horace stared down at his food in despair. Things were turning from bad to worse.

After dinner Horace walked up to his room. He still had another hour before he was meeting up with Milton. He closed the door behind him and sat down on the edge of his bed. Everything had fallen apart so fast. Anna was trapped back in Egypt with Meri and Tut, and now his parents were selling the farm.

Across from his desk was a tall shelf filled with comics, a couple of action figures, and a collection of books he'd been given over the years. As his eyes wandered across the dusty shelves—he hadn't read many of the books in years—he noticed one he'd barely remembered. A hardcover his grandfather had given him several birthdays ago. Horace felt curiously drawn to the old book. He reached out and grabbed its warped cover.

For the next hour he riffled through the pages. It was all about King Tut and the discovery of his tomb in 1922. It mentioned a little bit about the mystery surrounding his reign, and at the end even touched on his enigmatic father, Akhenaten.

From what Horace could piece together, Tut's family had had a complicated and strange history. Akhenaten had moved their family and the government to Amarna, a new city he'd built in the middle of Egypt. This change had been huge. Every Egyptian city was connected to a god. So, by creating his own city, Akhenaten had also created a new god, his own god. And that had been when, with a dramatic decree, he'd ended the worship of all the other gods and replaced them with one: Aten, the god of the sun.

Horace sat back for a moment. This was exactly what Meri had told them in Egypt. But why do that? Why risk everything when it was all going so well by outlawing the worship of other gods? And did any of this connect to the Benben Stone?

He kept reading. At the end of his seventeenth year of rule, Akhenaten had unexpectedly died, and his young son, Tut, had been left to run the country. Here, the story began to fray. From what Horace could tell, a strange set of circumstances had brought the boy pharaoh to the throne. His uncle had played some advisory role and then Tut had also died mysteriously. Yet nowhere in the book was there a single mention of any magical stones.

As Horace turned the page, a small newspaper clipping fell out. It was dated ten years earlier and described the announcement of a new exhibit at the museum. The Michigan Relics! These were the artifacts Anna and Milton had mentioned at lunch. The article went on to detail both the excitement of the exhibit as well as the controversy that surrounded the relics' authenticity.

At the bottom of the page Horace saw a faded black-and-white photograph of his grandfather standing in front of the exhibit, wearing a big smile. Behind him was a glass case full of the objects connected to the exhibit. However, that wasn't the strangest part. In the corner of the picture was an unmistakable granite pyramid. It was the Benben Stone.

CHAPTER SIXTEEN

Goose bumps covered Horace's arm. What was the Benben Stone doing in Niles?

He stared out the window at the evening sun and an overwhelming feeling filled his chest. Had his grandfather known about the magical stone?

From the first floor he heard the chimes of the clock. Horace snapped out of his daze. He'd totally lost track of time.

He ran down the stairs and into the kitchen. "Mom, I'm just going for a little bike ride."

"Okay, but be home before it's dark. Dad wants to watch a movie tonight."

"Sure, no problem." He bit down on his lip.

"Is everything okay?" she asked.

Horace just shrugged.

"I know it was hard to hear we might sell the farm."

"I just don't think Grandpa or Grandma would want us to sell it. Can't we figure out some way to keep it?"

"Listen, Horace, we're all doing our best. But how about this: I promise I won't let your uncle sell it unless we have absolutely no other options. Does that sound like a deal to you?"

"Okay."

"Now try not to think about it too much."

Horace feigned a smile. "Sure." Then he dashed out the door.

His bike rested against the plastic siding of the garage. The bike was old, its gold-and-black lettering faded and the leather seat full of cracks. He jumped on and was off.

Horace settled down into a rhythmic cadence of pedaling as he rode through the neighborhood and out past the edge of town. He was just about to get out of his seat for an extra boost of energy when he caught something out of the corner of his eye. He was approaching one of the town parks. He dismissed the first shape for a high-school student until he saw another shape, this one from the other side.

"Oh no . . ." Horace said to himself, swallowing nervously. It was Seth and his gang.

He had to make a quick decision. There was only one road past the Niles airport, which was on the way to the farm. If he turned around, there was a good chance Seth wouldn't see him, but he also might never get to the farm. He paused and looked ahead. He'd faced down Seth on the playground, but the streets of Niles were a whole other ball game. On top of it, Shadow was nowhere in sight.

He wasn't that far from the farm, maybe another half mile. He'd give it his best effort, or die trying. Horace stood up out of his seat and began to pedal at a furious pace, his head down.

For a brief moment he thought he might actually escape unscathed, but then he heard Seth's low baritone voice.

"Hey! Hey, Horace. What are you doing here?"

Horace looked back and now saw three kids appear out

of the bushes behind Seth.

"Hey, wait up, partner. What's the rush?"

Chancing another glance, Horace noticed Seth and his friends had already grabbed their bikes and were headed in his direction.

"Make this easier for yourself, Horace, and just give up," Seth chided. "The more we have to chase you, the worse it's going to be."

The second kid riding alongside Seth was pedaling extra hard and looked like he was going to try to jam a stick into Horace's tire. Horace wasn't an idiot; if the stick got in his spoke, he was destined for a painful fall, and an even more painful beating.

He continued to pedal as hard as he could, but the boy was gaining ground. A ditch ran alongside the road, and beyond that a line of trees. Now the kid was only half a tire's length away from Horace's bike.

The whole incident reminded Horace of those chariot races from Ancient Rome. It felt like he was in the giant hippodrome. He'd even seen videos about it, gladiators and warriors racing around the track, slamming into one another and battling for their lives. Suddenly the thought of the chariot races gave Horace an idea. It was gutsy and might cost him dearly, but it also might be his only chance against this kid. Seth and the rest of the gang were still a good five feet behind them.

The boy was starting to poke at his wheel. He was so close, Horace could see the pimples on his face. Horace waited for him to try again, and actually slowed down a touch to encourage another go at his back tire. Seth's friend pulled the stick back again, readying to throw it into the tire. At that second, Horace swung his handlebars hard to the left, driving his tire into the kid's bike. The force caught the boy totally off guard, and the next thing Horace knew, the boy was tumbling off his bike and slamming into the other two riders behind him.

Now Seth was the only one who remained. Somehow he'd avoided the collision. But Horace could see he was starting to labor under the long sprint.

The road still stretched another quarter mile before it reached the driveway to the farm.

Horace continued to pedal with all his might.

He could hear Seth's friend calling, "Leave him for now. We'll get him later."

"We're tired!" another shouted.

But Seth wasn't so easily persuaded. "No, I want this little rat. I'm not letting him go."

Seth was just starting to gain speed when, to Horace's relief, a car pulled onto the road ahead. The sudden appearance of headlights was all it took to get Seth to abandon his hunt.

"I'll get you, Horace!" shouted Seth, and he rode off toward the woods after his friends.

Horace was surprised when Milton's dad's head popped out from the driver's window. "Hey, Horace. How are you?"

"Good, Officer Williams."

"What are you doing out here? This seems like a long way from your house at this time of night."

Horace didn't want to tell him he was heading toward the farm. "Just getting some fresh air, I guess."

"Were those boys bothering you?" He nodded in the direction of Seth's gang.

"No, just saying hi."

"All right." He looked unconvinced, then continued, "By the way, have you seen Anna? Her parents are looking for her. She never came home after school. I've tried to call Milton, but he's not picking up his phone."

"Anna, ummm. I think she was finishing some homework with Milton at your house." Horace could start to feel his hands getting clammy.

"Oh, I'll be sure to tell her parents, then. Those two are always working on their homework together."

"Yeah," Horace nodded. "They are."

"Have a good night, but try to keep out of trouble," Officer Williams added, then headed down the road.

"I'll try."

Horace got on his bike and continued toward the farm.

chapter seventeen

"Run for it!" Horace grabbed Milton by the arm as they charged toward the city's shattered gates. They'd both gone through the portal at the farm without incident, but when they'd arrived through the obelisk in Amarna, it was as if Smenk's soldiers had been waiting for them.

Immediately one of the guards reached out to grab Milton by the robe, but with a single swipe of his forearm, Horace knocked him away. More shouting filled the street behind them as the two sidestepped another soldier.

Amarna already bore the deep scars of Smenk's attack. Discarded carts, smashed doors, and decapitated statues littered the streets. The pungent smell of burning wood and paper lingered. The boys took a few more turns through the ravaged streets in an effort to elude their pursuers before hiding at the end of a dark alley.

"That was a close call," said Milton between heavy breaths. "I thought the first guard had me until you gave him that forearm to the stomach."

Horace was surprised how easily they'd escaped the guards. "Yeah, that was close." Horace bit down on his lower lip. "It was weird, though. They seemed to know we were coming, but then they just let us go. Don't you think they should have put more effort into chasing us?"

"Well, just be grateful we escaped."

As the sounds of shouting grew louder, the two knelt even lower and started to plan their next move.

"We've got to get to the temple," Horace insisted. "I'm guessing that's where Anna and the others still are." Horace scanned the unfamiliar alley. "But I have no idea how to get there or even where we are."

Milton grinned. From his robe he pulled out a tightly rolled scroll. "I may have taken a little souvenir the last time we were here." Milton laid out the crumpled papyrus on the ground, and the two boys huddled around it. "I found it in that abandoned room."

"What is it?" asked Horace.

"It's a map of the whole city. Sorry about all the wrinkles. I tried to dry it out with my mom's hair dryer after the swim through the cisterns." There were a few missing sections from where the ink had dissolved, but the temple was an unmistakable rectangular structure in the center of the scroll.

"This is great!" answered Horace as he began to lay out their route on the map. "When we first came in through the obelisks, we ran to the right and then the left. So that would put us here." Horace pointed at the end of a narrow alley.

"Then we just need to circle around and try one of these side entrances." Milton traced out what seemed like the most direct path to the temple.

"I think you're right."

Milton nodded. "Then what are we waiting for? Let's go."

The two boys headed back down the narrow alleyway,

paused to make sure the coast was clear, and then ran across the road. Thankfully, there were no guards at this end of the street, and all the discarded debris provided plenty of cover. After a few more minutes and several close calls, one of which was a stray cat Milton almost tripped over, they made their way to what they thought was the entrance. But as soon as they arrived, they noticed a big problem.

"Ummm, I think we might have taken a wrong turn," said Horace in frustration. The supposed entrance was a ten-foot stone wall.

"I'm telling you, the temple is on the other side of this. See here on the map." Milton pointed adamantly. "We just need to get over this thing. Maybe we could build a ramp or pile this junk up."

There were giant stones all over the alley, but there was no way either of the boys had the strength or the size to lift them alone.

Horace looked down at the map to check their exact position again. "Do you think there's another way in?"

As the two boys stood there contemplating their dilemma, the shouting grew especially loud. They watched a group of soldiers chase a man past the alleyway.

"That guy looks like he's in a lot of trouble," commented Milton.

"Yeah, I wonder who it is," said Horace half to himself. "Maybe one of the priests."

Then the figure ran by again. Horace noted something strangely familiar about him. "I don't think that's a man. It looks like a kid."

And then the figure came sprinting into the alley, ducking into the far end. The soldiers ran right by.

"Is that—" Horace whispered to Milton.

"But how'd he get here?" interrupted Milton.

"He must have followed me up to the farm." Horace paused. "Should we help him?"

This time Milton shook his head in a simple response.

"But he could help us. He's big enough to move these stones."

Milton continued to shake his head. But Horace began to make his way slowly, step by step, toward the boy now crunched in a ball. He could hear a soft whimpering sound.

He whispered, "Hey, it's me, Horace."

The figure turned. "Horace!"

"Shhhhhhh . . ."

The expression on Seth's face was one of pure terror.

Horace tried to be reassuring. "It's okay." He paused. "But what are you doing here?"

"What am *I* doing here? What are you two idiots doing here? I followed you through that tree on the farm. I thought you had some secret clubhouse in there. Instead I find these guys with swords trying to kill me." Seth looked like he was ready to have a nervous breakdown.

Milton was now standing by Horace's side. "See, I told you we should have just left him here."

"What is this place?" asked Seth, ignoring Milton's comment.

Horace reached out a helping hand. "You're in Ancient Egypt."

"What?" Seth brushed away the hand, picked himself up, and put both of his arms out defensively.

"That would be correct. We might have to sacrifice you to the priests, though, since you're the biggest. That way there'd be more for them to feast upon," Milton said, instinctively ducking his head to avoid Seth's fist.

"Milton, enough joking around."

"You two better get me home, or I'll beat the snot out of you." Seth looked like he was starting to get back to his old self.

But the comment did remind Horace why they were here in the first place. "We've got to get into the temple." He pointed at the wall behind them.

"I'm not going in there."

"See, I told you. He's fine where he is," said Milton sarcastically.

More soldiers ran past the end of the street, and the three kids ducked low.

"We need to get over that wall, Seth, and I think you can help," said Horace.

"I'm not helping you." Seth crossed his arms.

"Well, you can sit here and pout, but if you don't help us, we aren't getting in there, and if we don't get in there, we aren't getting out of here."

"What's the worst that can happen to me if I stay here?" Seth pressed.

"Let me think." Milton made a mock gesture of actually pondering the question. "You could get captured by those guards, you could be captured, then jailed, or you could get tortured, jailed, then killed. Get the idea?"

Seth glanced down at the ground, seeming to process the seriousness of his predicament.

"Listen, Seth, we need your help," Horace pleaded. "Anna needs your help."

Seth's brow furrowed. "Anna? What is she doing here?"

"She's trapped," Horace said.

The realization of Anna's being here, the sound of more shouting guards, and the fading light of the day seemed to hit Seth all at once.

"Fine. But when we get back to Niles, you two better never mention this."

Milton rolled his eyes. "As if I couldn't wait to get home and tell everyone I hung out with you in Ancient Egypt."

They waited a few more minutes until the guards found a new distraction. The three boys then created a line and began piling everything they could find in the alley against the wall: stones, fragments of wood, even clay jars.

Seth proved an invaluable ally, moving the biggest stones and creating a wide foundation. Soon the three of them had created quite a tower.

Milton finally placed the last clay jar onto their pile. Sweat dripped from his face as he stepped back and examined the teetering ladder. "This doesn't look safe enough for a mouse to climb."

"You've got to try," insisted Horace, and Milton began to climb. But even with only the partial weight of Milton's body, the whole contraption tilted to the right. Milton froze as the pile creaked its way back to center.

"Keep going," Horace urged. "Seth, hold the bottom." Milton took another deep breath and resumed his ascent. Slowly, he climbed higher and higher. After another anxious minute, Milton finally reached the top. "I made it!" he shouted down.

"Seth, you're next."

Seth looked at Horace and shook his head. "I'm not doing this."

"We don't have a choice, Seth. You've got to go."

Seth jumped on the first jar. The pile teetered again, far

worse than it had for Milton, and a few pieces even came tumbling down. Horace raced to brace the bottom, and Milton grabbed the top. Timidly, Seth ascended the pile.

Horace took one glance back and saw a soldier approaching from down the alley. "There they are!" the soldier shouted.

Without pausing, Horace turned toward the wall again, and nimbly climbed up the pile of debris. For once, it was an advantage to be small. Before he knew it, he was standing on the ledge alongside the two other boys.

"Help me knock this down!" yelled Horace.

Quickly, Milton scurried over and gave the pile a hard jab with his legs.

The guard beneath them was struggling to climb the pile, but his weight combined with Milton's forceful kick sent the whole thing crumbling down. The guard turned and ran down the alleyway, shouting for more help.

Horace scanned the narrow ledge in both directions. "Let's get out of here."

"Yeah, yeah, let's get out of here," said Seth. "I don't want to stand up here forever."

Could their tough companion have a little fear of heights? Horace smiled to himself before nodding.

"Let's see." Milton scanned the map again. "I think we can use this to get over to the West Wing. That's where we saw Anna last. Remember?"

Horace agreed and began leading the three of them along the narrow width of the wall. Seth stayed in the middle while Milton brought up the rear. The wall wasn't built for walking. It was for defense. In several places the stone narrowed, and in others, it simply crumbled under their feet. Twice Horace had to grab Seth to catch him from falling, and once Seth's quick hand kept Milton from plunging to his own death.

"I think we're close," Horace noted as the buildings changed from yellow limestone to black granite. From his tour with Tut and his escape with Milton, Horace knew this was the site of the forbidden West Wing, where only the priests were allowed.

"Over there—look. We might be able to get down." Horace pointed at a sloping section of the wall. The base was much wider than the top. It looked like the slide at the school playground, just a lot steeper.

The three of them inched across the wall to the sloping section.

"I'll go first," Horace volunteered.

"No way. What if you break a leg?" protested Milton.

"Let him go," suggested Seth. "That will teach him for bringing us to this crazy place."

"Listen, if Horace gets hurt, none of us is getting out of here. He's the only one who knows how to get home."

"Okay, then we can all go together," said Horace, trying to calm the growing tension between his two companions.

Seth took a deep breath and nodded. It looked like a dangerously long way, but there didn't appear to be any other options.

"Ready?" Horace paused as the others got into position alongside him. "One . . . two . . . three . . . jump!"

The three boys squeezed hands as they leaped off the ledge and skimmed down the sloping surface. Horace's skin burned against the hard stone of the wall as the gravel rapidly approached from below. Then, in a sudden cloud of dirt and dust, they hit the ground.

Horace scanned his body quickly for broken bones before looking around at his two companions. "Is everyone okay?"

"I'm fine." Seth brushed a chunk of dirt from his robe. The fall seemed to quiet his protesting, at least for the time being.

"Me too." Milton tightened his threaded belt.

Horace looked up at the wall. It must have been fifteen feet high. "I can't believe we did that."

"And survived," added Milton.

"There's got to be a door around here that can lead us into the temple."

The two boys followed Horace to another passageway, this one lined with giant columns and flickering torches. As they walked toward the complex's inner core, the light began to disappear, and the torches became fewer and farther between. Scared of their own shadows, they made their way to a flight of stairs that descended into darkness.

"This is going to take forever if we keep walking around like this. The temple's half the size of the city. I think we should split up," suggested Horace.

"I don't know. That doesn't sound like a good idea," said Milton.

Seth didn't say anything. The thought of walking around alone in this place appeared to terrify him.

"I think it's our only shot. We need to find Anna fast," Horace insisted. "You two, stay together. I've been here before. Maybe we'll find Tut, too."

Milton cringed at the thought of being partnered with Seth.

But Seth was still caught up on Horace's other words. "Who did you say?"

"Yeah, we're in Ancient Egypt at the time of King Tut," Milton whispered. "And if we don't help him and Anna, everything you've ever learned about Ancient Egypt is going to be destroyed."

The words seemed to make the seriousness of their task even more real.

"But what if something happens to one of us?" Milton finally asked Horace.

Horace didn't even want to entertain the possibility. "No matter what, meet at the temple gates in an hour."

"Do you need this?" Seth held out his slingshot in an unexpected gesture.

"Are you sure?"

"I always keep an extra one around." He pulled out a second slingshot.

Horace laughed, for the first time glad to have Seth as his partner.

chapter eighteen

Wandering alone through the cool, dark hallways of the western sanctuary, Seth's slingshot in hand, Horace took the beetle out of his pocket. Twice he'd ducked into random rooms and even a hallway to sidestep the pursuit of soldiers.

At the end of a particularly long passage, he stopped. There was a group of guards in a heated discussion. He was about to make a run for it in the other direction, when shouting filled the hall behind him. Horace quickly slipped into the darkness of a nearby doorway. A soldier came charging by.

"There's been a break-in!" the man shouted. "The

guards at the gate say a group of men have breached the walls and are trying to free the prisoners. We found a pile of debris they used, and we've got orders to send reinforcements. You three, come with me."

"But what about the—" The sound of an explosion drowned out the other soldier's words.

The men went running past Horace, along the same path he'd just come from. It was too dangerous to go back now and, clearly, there was something important ahead.

He just had to get past one remaining guard. Inspired by what he'd seen Seth do so many times on the playground, he reached into his robe and pulled out the slingshot. There was only one stone to use. Ever so carefully, he placed the beetle into the soft pouch. With a shaking hand, he stretched the cord as far as it would go. Finally, after lining it up just right, he released the pouch. In a flash of light, the beetle flew across the corridor, and with a loud thump, the guard fell to the ground.

Horace ran forward and, to his great relief, found the guard still breathing but knocked out cold; the beetle was lying on the ground next to him. He picked it up and then turned to the doorway. It was the same room he and his friends had been trapped in when Smenk had tortured the priests. Was Anna in there?

Slowly, he peeked his head around the heavy curtain. It was too difficult to see anything, but as Horace passed inside, a chill swept over him. The room was empty. Horace noticed a doorway on the opposite side, something he hadn't spotted the first time he'd been there. Slowly, he walked to the door. It opened onto a tunnel that descended into darkness. A strange sound was coming from within its depths, like heavy breathing. Could it be his friends?

He hadn't gone more than a few feet before the light behind him was swallowed up. The tunnel was so dark, Horace couldn't imagine how anyone could navigate it without hurting themselves. His foot smacked against the edge of the wall, and he realized he'd reached a junction. The path split in two directions. The faint light of another torch illuminated a gruesome trail of small bones ahead. The other corridor was blanketed in darkness. He decided to try his luck with the lit passage, despite the unsettling remains. At least that way he'd see if anything jumped out and tried to kill him, he thought.

A few more steps and then a giant breeze swept through the tunnel. The torchlight went out.

"Great," he said to himself in frustration. He couldn't see a thing, and the tunnel was creepy—much creepier than he'd realized. Maybe this wasn't such a good idea.

But he pulled out the beetle and, sure enough, it began to glow blue. A dozen more steps brought him to the edge of something even more unexpected. Resting in the center of a room, circled by burning torches, was a single black stone set upon a small altar.

"The Benben Stone!" Horace gasped. Smenk must have moved it beneath the temple. But why down here?

Suddenly Horace smelled the strong odor of rotting meat. It wasn't Smenk or Eke or even another soldier. An amber mane shimmered in the torchlight, and the source of the heavy breathing revealed itself. A lion emerged from the darkness. This was what Tut had warned him about on his first visit. How could he have forgotten? The priests kept creatures deep within the temple to protect their treasures. This must be one of those animals, and it was guarding the Benben Stone.

Then it began to speak.

You have come for the stone. The lion raised the corner of its mouth to reveal a set of long, sharp teeth. *And to help your friends.* His lips weren't moving, but Horace could hear the words in his head. *If you answer the riddle correctly, the stone will be yours, but if not . . .* The mouth flared open again, dripping with desire.

Horace squeezed the beetle and swallowed. "I don't want the stone; I was just looking for my friends. Do you know where they are?" he asked.

The lion began to circle Horace. *Friendship, such a dangerous human trait.*

"Are they safe?" Horace insisted.

The lion's eyes rolled back in its head like something out of a horror movie. Then, just as quickly, the pupils reappeared. *Your friends, yes, I see them. Three of them are in prison, and the other two have just been caught.*

"What?" Horace was biting down on his lip so hard, he could taste the metallic tinge of blood. He needed to get out of here and help them. For a moment he wondered if he could outrun the beast. Its thick hind legs suggested definitely not.

If what the lion said was true, Milton and Seth had already been captured and now were at Smenk's mercy just like Anna, Tut, and Meri. And if he ran back into the temple, that same fate could await him. But if he stayed and answered the riddle incorrectly, he might also get killed.

He considered the shimmering surface of the stone, and sensed an ancient magic. Maybe the Benben Stone was his only hope. Maybe its magic could help him free his friends and get all of them out of there alive.

Finally Horace looked the terrifying creature in the eyes: there was no other option. "Okay, I'll answer the riddle."

Good. Now let us begin. The lion paced in an even wider circle around Horace. *Once, there was a great pharaoh. He had all the wealth in the world and the largest palace in the land. Yet he still wasn't fulfilled. He called his wisest advisors together and told them to find him something that would make him happy when he was sad, and sad when he was happy. The advisors were fearful of disappointing their ruler, but they also knew nothing of the sort existed. For a year they scoured the countryside, looking for an answer in the villages, the temples, even the sacred tombs, but there was nothing. Finally they returned to the palace.*

"Our lord," they replied. "We have looked everywhere, but there is nothing that can bring happiness when you are sad, and sadness when you are happy."

The pharaoh sent them away.

The men spent another year searching. They returned again, empty-handed. The pharaoh grew angry at their failure and gave them one last warning. "This is your final chance. Find me something that will make me happy when I'm sad and sad when I'm happy, or you will all be banished from my kingdom."

Another year passed. On the last day of the last month of this third year, a strange turn of events occurred. The men were on their way to the palace, when a boy overheard their conversation. He interrupted. "I know the answer to your riddle. Let me speak to the pharaoh."

The men told the young boy to go away. They didn't have time to waste. But the boy continued to follow them.

One of the men turned to the boy. "Tell us, then. What is it?"

The boy refused. "I will tell only the pharaoh."

Finally, after much debate, the men agreed to take the boy to the pharaoh, too desperate now to argue.

When the pharaoh saw the young boy standing before his throne, he started laughing, then turned to his advisors. "A child has come to tell me what not even the wisest men in this court can answer?" They begged the pharaoh to give the boy a chance to speak and hoped whatever he said would save their lives. Finally the boy stepped forward and offered a simple answer. The lion paused and looked deep into Horace's eyes. *What did he say?*

Beads of sweat ran down Horace's neck.

I need an answer, the lion growled, and stepped closer to Horace.

In his mind, Horace saw the clock in his grandfather's office, the towering obelisks of Amarna, the clay tablets in Ay's classroom. For so many sleepless nights, he'd wondered why he'd been given the beetle. He had always thought it must be some kind of terrible mistake, and now his inability to answer this riddle felt like proof.

The lion tensed its muscles, readying to pounce.

Horace was just about to surrender, when he heard the sound of slowly dripping water from somewhere deep in the room. It almost sounded like the ticking of a clock. How quickly each day had gone by since school had first started. How fast his dad had ripped off the calendar for September and replaced it with the pumpkin-covered page that was October. Cleveland was just a memory, and now Niles was his new home. He saw himself sitting with his father that night he'd first found out about his grandfather's death. They were on the bed. "I know it's hard for you to hear, Horace, but this, too, will pass in time. Everything changes in time, even these tough moments. Out of them will grow something good," his dad had said.

At first Horace thought it was just a silly memory. And then he realized it was the answer. His dad had given him the answer. "That's it! I know what would make someone happy when they're sad and sad when they're happy."

The lion's expression glimmered with curiosity.

"Everything changes in *time*. It's true! The good,

the bad. Everything changes in time." Horace answered triumphantly. "The answer is time."

To Horace's surprise, the creature took a step backward.

You have solved the riddle, and now not even I can stand in your way. Place the beetle in the stone and you will be granted a memory, one you have been wishing to see, young Keeper. One that will answer a pressing question within your heart. And with that, the lion disappeared into the darkness.

He'd done it. The Benben Stone was his! All doubt, failure, and insecurity disappeared. He had recovered what Smenk had stolen, and he would use it to save his friends.

The beetle vibrated strangely in his hand, pulling him forward. Its blue light mixed with the deep black and purple hues of the Benben Stone, illuminating the outlines of strange symbols and writing.

Just a few feet from the gold platform, the energy between the two stones grew even more intense, like a pair of giant magnets pulling at each other. Horace slowly placed the beetle into a small, oval hole in the middle of the stone. He knew exactly what memory he'd wish for. The same thing he'd wished for every day and night for the past weeks: to see his grandfather one last time.

The Benben Stone began to pulse. A wave of energy passed through his arm and swelled in his lungs. From the center of the stone emerged a bluish-purple light, rising above the stone. Horace wondered if a new portal was about to open, but then the light began to take a strange shape, a holographic image that filled the entire room.

At first Horace thought the shapes were reflections of the shadows in the room, but then he started to recognize faces. He saw his mom and dad. Himself as a baby. Another flash and a scene of his sisters when they were younger; another, and then his grandfather, kneeling in the garden with someone. He was with Horace, but Horace must have been no older than two or three. It was one of his first trips to Michigan. With a final flash, there standing at the farm were three new shapes—Herman, his grandfather, and . . . Smenk? They were in the open field near the tree and his grandfather was holding the Benben Stone in his hands.

Smenk lifted his staff, and a bolt of lightning flew

from the tip and exploded at his grandfather's feet. "Don't be a fool! You're helpless against my power!" Another bolt flew from the staff, this time striking his grandfather in the hand. He winced but continued to hold the stone.

"Give it to me!"

Two more lightning bolts leaped from the staff. They hit his grandfather's hands, first the right, then the left.

"Never!"

Smenk gripped the staff again, this time with both hands, and raised it above his head. "Now you will die!" he roared. With a brilliant flash of blinding light, he lifted Horace's grandfather and the Benben Stone high into the air.

"Before I kill you, I want you to know I will find your friends, and one by one I will kill them, too." And then, with the same flash of light he'd used to lift his grandfather up into the air, Smenk slammed him down upon the ground. He lifted the Benben Stone into his arms, looked over his shoulder, and vanished into the portal.

A second shadow walked over to the dark silhouette of Horace's grandfather. It was Herman. He dropped to his knees. "What should we do? He has it."

His grandfather reached into his pocket and pulled out the scarab beetle. "Find Horace."

CHAPTER NINETEEN

Horace stepped back, and the light from the two stones flickered. The beetle popped out and flew into his hand. Watching Smenk kill his grandfather was the worst thing he'd ever seen. Worse than the afternoon he first learned of his grandfather's death. Touching the Benben Stone had burned the memory of the murder not just into his mind, but into his skin, his bones, and even his heart.

The stone did have magical powers. It seemed to hold memories. *Yet why would these be so important to Smenk?* wondered Horace. How could memories be wielded as an all-encompassing power?

He wasn't going to wait around to find out. And he

wasn't just going to leave the Benben Stone lying on this altar for Smenk to use later. Horace realized it wasn't enough just to help his friends. He had to steal the stone too. It would be justice for what had happened to his grandfather.

Horace began to pull at the stone's smooth edges. He was surprised by its weight for such a small object.

He squeezed with his fingers and lifted with his legs. When the stone separated from the platform, it got much lighter. Horace almost fell over from the sudden change. There was a magnetic connection between the two. He steadied himself and turned toward the exit.

"Where do you think you're going?"

Horace froze.

"Stealing my stone, are we?" Smenk's unmistakable silhouette appeared out of the shadows.

Horace wondered if Smenk had watched his whole exchange with the lion.

Smenk pointed the glowing red tip of his staff directly at Horace. "Put it back."

Horace didn't move.

"I'm not going to repeat myself."

Finally Horace slowly placed the Benben Stone on the altar.

Smenk walked toward him. "So you are the Keeper of the scarab beetle." His expression held both contempt and surprise. "I expected someone a little bit"—he paused—"older."

Horace felt the beetle in his palm while he stared into Smenk's cold, cruel eyes. The same eyes that had shown no mercy to his grandfather.

Smenk's gaze moved to Horace's hand. "Give that to me!" And in a single motion he snatched the beetle and placed it on the Benben Stone.

For a moment Horace feared he was about to witness the true power of both stones under Smenk's control, but nothing happened. Smenk couldn't get the beetle to fit into the keyhole. He took it off the Benben Stone and tried again, even more forcefully. Nothing.

Horace started inching backward, wondering if he might be able to escape.

"I must access the power of the stone!" Smenk cried,

smashing the beetle against the granite surface. "Does this child have some power not even I possess?"

He turned and caught sight of Horace edging his way toward the door. "Where do you think you're going?" he said again.

Smenk marched over to Horace and slapped the beetle into his hand. "If you have the power, you are going to open the stone for me." With icy fingers, Smenk shoved him toward the altar. "Use it!"

Horace didn't know what power Smenk was talking about. When he connected with the Benben Stone, he'd only revealed memories of his grandfather. What was important about those memories?

Smenk seemed to read his thoughts. "You foolish child. Don't you realize within this stone resides not just the memories of all those who have ever touched it, but also the secrets of the ancients who created it? This stone holds the hidden history of the world." With each word, Smenk's face took on a greater intensity. "It is a window into the ultimate secrets of the universe and their magical powers. And you will access them for me. All of them."

"But I don't even know how I did it," Horace pleaded nervously. "I was just messing around earlier." He squeezed the beetle tightly and bit down on his lip. "I'll die if I have to, but I'm not going to help you." Horace closed his eyes.

"You think I'm going to kill you?" Smenk snickered as he pointed his staff at Horace. "What good would that do?" He moved his staff above Horace's head. "But I will kill them."

Seth, Milton, Anna, Meri, and Tut stood at the room's entrance between a group of armed guards. Their robes were badly torn and covered in dirt.

"Horace!" Anna shouted.

A guard jabbed her in the side. "No talking!"

"Don't touch her!" Horace yelled.

A bolt of light erupted from Smenk's staff, striking Anna in the leg. She fell to the ground with a scream. "If you want your friends to live, you'd better open the stone."

Horace knew he had no options.

"Do it!" yelled Smenk. "Now!"

Slowly, Horace approached the stone. He stared at the markings. What could he draw out of this stone that

Smenk wanted so badly? He didn't know any of its secrets. He'd just stumbled on it while searching for his friends.

When he placed the beetle into it, he felt a deep pulse move through his whole body, just like the last time. A purple haze soon filled the room.

The first memories that came out of the stone weren't remarkable. They were ordinary images of Horace's childhood, pictures of his sisters playing. Each picture went back earlier and earlier in his life. One even showed him sleeping in a crib.

"I want more," Smenk urged him. "Go deeper into the stone. Find the memories of the ancient ones, the builders of this sacred land, and the secrets of the Keepers."

Horace kept his hand pressed firmly against the stone. Strange, dark images began to surface: flashes of war, a city on fire, and a fortress high on a mountain.

"Yes . . ." Smenk hissed. "Now the memories are awakening."

Horace noticed the color of the stone had changed from purple to green. He wanted to remove the beetle, but the threat of what Smenk might do to his friends forced him on.

Temples rising and falling in the sands appeared above the stone, craftsmen measuring out vast cities and building intricate tombs. The images dissolved.

"Yes, yes, the secrets of the builders," Smenk said behind him.

Anna's voice pierced through the fog. "Stop!" She was pleading. "Horace, stop before you reveal too much."

But Horace didn't, or couldn't, stop.

The next scene was a strange ceremony in the desert. Nine men stood in a circle chanting under the stars. Horace watched as a great light erupted from a stone at the center of the circle into the night sky. It was the Benben Stone.

"More, more. Show me the hidden knowledge!" Smenk shouted.

Another wave of light exploded from the stone, which was now pulsing red. Horace couldn't see any images because the flashes of blinding color were so intense.

"Horace!" He could make out Tut's faint voice. "Don't do this."

And Horace suddenly realized he had to stop. Images

were pouring out of the stone now. Frightening images of wars and death and entire cities burning to the ground. Each seemed to get more and more violent. The sounds of people screaming echoed throughout the room.

Somehow Horace had to gain control of the stone. If he was a Keeper, there must be a way to bend this sacred object to his will. He had manifested the memory of his grandfather through a simple wish—maybe there were other memories locked in the stone that could help him. Maybe someone else's memories in the stone could be accessed. Memories Smenk did not want to be revealed?

Horace closed his eyes but kept his hand on the stone. He was no longer looking at the images; instead he was channeling his deepest desire into the stone.

Smenk noticed immediately. "What are you doing?" he yelled. "Go back to the other memories."

The image was hazy at first, but then it became clearer. Projected above the stone were two young men, one might have even been a teenager, standing in an open courtyard.

Meri was the first to recognize the older of the two figures. "Ay!"

The Ay in the memory spoke, "The Order has made up its mind."

The younger of the two was Smenk. He was pleading. "Let me try again."

"There is nothing you can do. The gift of the Time Keepers does not run in your veins like your brother's."

"There must be another way," Smenk begged.

"There is no other way. The decision is final."

The scene suddenly changed, and this time Smenk was much older. He was standing across from another figure.

Tut yelled, "Father!"

Akhenaten stood brazenly as Smenk pointed his staff at him. "Put it down."

"Always telling me what to do, older brother. You think you are so smart, you think you are so talented because they choose you and not me. Well, there are others who recognize my talents besides your foolish order of priests. There are others who will celebrate your death and consider me a great hero."

"My death will change nothing, Smenk. The memory of Amarna can never be erased."

Smenk spat, "Oh, that's where you are wrong. This city, your name, your family. I will make sure they're all destroyed. Not even the gods will remember you."

Akhenaten remained calm. "You can kill me, but it will not give you the power you seek."

"Yes, it will. I'll find your precious stone, and it will give me what the Keepers refused. And then I will be even more powerful than you and your crippled son."

Horace watched in horror as Smenk raised his staff.

"No!" Tut's piercing cry helped Horace know what he needed to do.

With a powerful force, Horace yanked the beetle from the Benben Stone, breaking the connection.

"Stop! Stop! Put that back!" Smenk shrieked. "I want the knowledge of the Keepers. And you defied me, you naive boy. Now you will face the same death as your grandfather and Akhenaten." Smenk sent a bolt of light directly at Horace.

He ducked just in time, and the bolt struck the Benben Stone. But rather than destroying it, the stone lit up even brighter. The shock wave from the bolt shook the room violently, sending giant chunks of plaster to the ground. The force had also knocked Smenk off his feet.

Tut and Seth used the momentary distraction to attack the guards holding them.

This was their chance. Horace grabbed the Benben Stone and made a break toward the doorway.

From the floor, Smenk fired at Horace. The bolts just missed him, ricocheting off the columns along the outer edge of the room. Between the Benben Stone's shock wave and Smenk's shots, the whole place seemed to be caving in.

"Horace!" Anna shouted from the ramp. "Run for it! The temple is collapsing!" Seth had managed to pry one of the spears from the guards and was using it to hold them back.

Horace sprinted under the collapsing supports.

"Come back here!" Smenk yelled over the din of crashing stone. "Come back here with that stone!"

"Run!" Anna shouted again.

Horace made it up to the ramp where his friends had somehow escaped serious injury. The guards were pinned under massive chunks of fallen ceiling, and Smenk was crawling across the ground as the temple collapsed around him. His eyes were a blaze of fire.

"No!" he yelled as Horace turned and ran.

chapter twenty

The kids emerged from the darkness of the crumbling temple and spotted the obelisks that marked their exit out of the city. One obelisk lay on the ground, and the other was trembling violently.

Horace wasted no time slamming the beetle against the remaining one. Immediately a blue portal opened in its base.

"Watch your head!" he shouted as his friends raced through.

The power released from the Benben Stone had unseated the very foundation of the city. Everything was falling around them.

Horace scanned the ruins of what was once a beautiful

city, and then slipped into the portal with the beetle in one hand and the Benben Stone under his arm.

"We made it," Horace said, relieved to be back at the farm.

Anna was hobbling across the yard, grasping her leg, Meri by her side. Seth had dropped the spear but still carried his slingshot. And Milton had his arm draped around Tut's shoulder, trying to catch his breath after the exhausting escape. While they all had bumps and bruises, everyone was okay.

"That was a close call," said Horace as he tried to regain his bearings. On the horizon, he could see the edge of the setting sun.

Anna joined in. "I can't believe what you did down there, Horace. It was like you tapped into Smenk's own memories and brought out some of his deepest insecurities. You should have seen the expression of fear on his face when those scenes appeared. It drove him crazy."

"Yeah," added Milton, "thank goodness you were able to duck those bolts from his staff."

Even Seth was impressed. "That was the most insane

fireworks display I've ever seen."

"Thanks. I still don't really understand it, but before you arrived, Smenk had tried to open the stone himself. I guess when he touched it, he imparted all his own memories in the process, both the good and the bad," answered Horace.

"Smenk was always jealous of my father, but I never imagined he was the one who killed him," said Tut. He was deeply upset.

"He must have thought getting the Benben Stone would give him that same power," added Horace.

"Yes," said Meri. "But you said the stone wouldn't open for him. That's because even with the key, he was still missing something."

Horace wondered what he possessed that Smenk didn't have.

A noise by the house caught their attention, and everyone turned to see a man coming around the corner. Horace recognized the hat and overcoat; he was the prospective buyer. But his uncle wasn't anywhere in sight.

"Kids, are you okay? I heard voices in the yard while I

was on the other side of the house."

"Who's that?" Milton whispered to Horace.

"He's the guy trying to buy our farm," Horace answered.

"What's he doing here at night?" Anna asked.

Horace didn't have an answer.

"Oh my, you look so dirty. Here, let me help you." The man started patting the mud off Horace's shirt. "That must be heavy. I can take it." He lifted the Benben Stone right out of a stunned Horace's arms.

Then the man removed his hat.

Horace gasped. "What are you doing here?"

Eke threw his coat off, and Horace was struck by how much taller he looked. In one hand was a crook. "Thought I was crippled, that I couldn't carry the stone. That it's too heavy for me. A little hunching and limping fool the best of them." In the other hand he revealed the beetle.

Horace checked his now-empty pocket where he'd been carrying the beetle. His thoughts were swimming in circles. Had Eke pickpocketed him when he was patting the dirt off his shoulders?

Eke grinned. "See how everything works out in the

end?"

"But what are you doing here? How did you get through the portal?" asked Horace.

"Didn't your grandfather ever teach you to lock the door behind you?"

"You'll never get away with this," Tut declared.

"I already have." He smiled back. "And so you don't try to follow me . . ." Flashes of red light flew from his crook. One hit Tut in the chest, another caught Anna in the arm, and three more sent Milton, Meri, and Seth to the ground.

Horace was the only one left standing. What was he going to do? He thought he had stopped Smenk. He'd tried to save Tut. But Eke was about to undo everything they'd achieved in Egypt. How had he dropped his guard so easily? His body started to sway from side to side, and his head felt incredibly light, as if a giant pool of water were rising around him. His ears filled with a buzzing sound. He tensed his muscles, ready to charge Eke.

"Don't be so foolish." Eke pointed his black staff at Horace as he walked over to the tree, where the portal was still open. Horace could see the tip of Eke's staff beginning to glow brighter.

"I won't be taking any more chances with you, young Keeper. I had my suspicions when I first saw you in the temple, but Smenk wouldn't listen to me. Well, he was wrong and now I'm the one with the Benben Stone." Eke raised his staff higher.

Then, out of the corner of his eye, Horace saw it. The shape was almost undetectable as it dove out of the tree. Eke didn't see the falcon until it was too late. The bird dug its sharp talons into his face.

"My eyes!" he screamed.

Shadow was relentless, clawing his skin. "Get it off me!" Eke yelled. "Get this bird off me!"

Horace couldn't believe it. The force of Shadow's attack was driving Eke backward step by step toward the open portal. Eke dropped the beetle, then the Benben Stone, as he desperately tried to keep the falcon at bay. Finally, with one loud screech, Shadow dove full speed into Eke's chest, pushing him right into the open portal.

Stunned, Horace stared at the empty spot where Eke had been.

He hesitantly walked over to pick up the beetle and the Benben Stone. "Thanks, Shadow," he said. "You're a lifesaver."

The bird chirped in response and hopped into the air.

Suddenly a bright light flashed from the tree and sent Horace to his knees, bracing for another attack.

But it wasn't Eke returning through the portal. It was Herman walking out of the tree. He was carrying a burlap bag over his shoulder.

"Herman!" Horace shouted.

"Horace, you're safe." The two embraced in a warm hug.

"Am I glad to see you."

Herman looked equally relieved. "I was worried I was too late."

"You almost were," answered Horace in frustration. "Where have you been? Eke was waiting for us here."

"I can't believe you held your own against both Smenk and Eke. And retrieved the Benben Stone," Herman said in amazement. "I was with the Order looking for a safe place for the stone."

Anna was hobbling across the yard. Seth was also up and moving, and he ran over to help her. "Are you okay?" Seth looked down at her injured leg.

"Don't worry. He just nicked me." She covered the gash Eke's blast had left.

Horace spotted Milton quietly grasping his side, breathing heavily. He rushed over.

"Who was that? That guy nearly killed me."

"Eke," answered Horace. "He was Smenk's henchman." Horace still couldn't figure out how Eke had been using the portal as well.

"You better not sell him this farm." Milton paused, picking himself up with Horace's help. "He's totally nuts!"

Tut was lying in a ball on the ground. Meri was standing next to him. Herman walked over and felt his wrist. He hesitated for a moment, searching for a pulse, and then looked up. Herman reached into his pocket and poured a small bottle of green liquid between Tut's open lips. Tut's fingers twitched, and then in the next second he opened his eyes.

"He'll be okay," Herman said. "You kids probably have

many questions, but you'll have to wait a little while to have them answered. We need to get your friends back to Egypt. They can't stay on this side of the portal any longer."

"You know Tut and Meri too?" Horace asked.

"Of course."

"But you can't send them back to Amarna where Eke is. He'll try to kill them again!" protested Milton.

"Don't worry. Eke's not in Egypt," Herman answered.

"What do you mean?" asked Horace.

"Shadow sent him to a place where he can't get to Tut."

"But what about Smenk? He's still in Amarna," Anna said.

"There is no more Amarna. And it will be centuries before Smenk's body is discovered beneath the sands of the city he destroyed."

"And the priests? Ay?" Horace wondered aloud.

"They're on their way to Thebes, where they must help heal a fractured country." Herman paused. "And Tut and Meri need to join them there as king and queen."

At that moment, Shadow circled high overhead, a glittering silhouette in the moonlight, then descended onto Horace's shoulder.

Seth flinched. "The falcon?"

"Take care of her while I'm gone, Horace. She's a good friend and a great messenger. If you need anything, Shadow knows where to find me." Then his voice hardened. "But you mustn't ignore my orders again. Traveling through the portal is unsafe. And the knowledge of your scarab beetle must be kept secret." Herman reached out his arms. "Now, Horace, I must also take the Benben Stone."

"But my grandfather had the stone. Why can't we keep it here?" Horace was confused. He had fought so hard to bring it back to Niles. He had risked his life to save the stone. And now Herman was just going to take it. "Haven't I proved I can guard the stone?"

"You have, Horace." Herman nodded. "You've shown courage and strength beyond your years and beyond what the Order ever expected. It's not you I'm worried about." Herman walked over and opened the brown burlap bag. "This is bigger than you know, Horace. There are other forces at work, even greater and more dangerous than Eke and Smenk. To keep the stone here would only draw them to Niles."

Horace bit down on his lip. Herman was probably right. He had witnessed through the Benben Stone what had happened to his grandfather. It wasn't hard to imagine what other wicked people might come looking for it, even in Niles.

Reluctantly, he set the stone inside the bag.

Then Herman took Tut and Meri by the hand. "Now, Horace, after we've walked through, place the beetle in the light. Turn it to the right, clockwise, and its magic will seal the portal until it is ready to be opened again by either you or another Keeper."

"There's more than one portal?"

Herman laughed. "Of course, Horace! And when you're ready, we'll explore a whole other world." He turned to Tut and Meri. "Ready?"

They both nodded.

"Good luck, Meri," said Anna.

"And be careful, Tut," Milton added. They all knew what Milton meant. They'd read the history books, and they knew Tut died young.

Horace walked over and gave Tut a big hug good-bye. "Thanks for everything," he said with a smile. "You're already a great king."

Tut grinned. "You're not a bad Time Keeper, either. Keep an eye on that beetle. I might need your help again someday."

Herman turned to the remaining group. "You have to understand that none of us can stop what will happen to Tut—or to anyone. But you protected the beetle and you saved the Benben Stone." He turned toward Horace. "Your grandfather would be proud."

With that, Tut gave one final wave, and Herman led him and Meri into the light. Horace placed the beetle against the tree and sealed the portal.

He felt Shadow leap off his shoulder, then looked down at the beetle in his hand. It was still glowing bright blue. Horace knew his dad was right: his grandfather was with him. He'd always been there. In the depths of his heart, his grandfather's voice echoed, and his memory glowed.

Horace nodded as he looked over at Anna, Seth, and

Milton still standing around the tree.

The plan had actually worked.

chapter twenty-one

The next day it felt strange to Horace to know Tut was in Egypt, struggling to bring the people together after his coronation, while Horace was safe in Niles. From his reading, he now knew Tut would soon turn from his father's god and return to the old gods, in the hopes of healing the scarred kingdom.

Horace also knew the threat of the farm being sold was real. Soon his uncle would clean up the mess in the yard and bring by more buyers to look at the property.

In the morning his dad took his sisters to soccer, and his mom offered to take Horace to the nursing home to visit Grandma. It would be the first time he'd seen her since his grandfather's death, and he was happy to have the opportunity to be with her again.

As they walked down the hall of the nursing home, the pungent smell of cleaning supplies and bleach filled Horace's nostrils. They passed several rooms. Each one was small and had a bed, a desk, and in some cases, a TV. He saw a nurse helping a woman into a wheelchair, and in another room an older man slumped forward, staring at a television with a fuzzy screen.

Horace recognized his grandma's room by the family pictures hanging outside the door. His heart skipped a beat when he saw one particularly weathered photograph of his grandparents standing in front of the farm. Just a few months ago they had sat on their porch, laughing with each other. And now one was here, and the other . . . Horace felt a twinge of shame. If his uncle sold the farm, his grandma would be stuck in this place forever.

His mom led him inside, where his grandma and a nurse sat on the bed. Horace noticed a change in her appearance already. Her gray hair was thinner, and her eyes had lost the mischievous glint that had always made her appear younger than she was. Grandpa used to tease Grandma about her eyes, saying when he saw them twinkle, he knew he was in for trouble.

The nurse looked over at Horace. "You must be Amelia's grandson. She has been asking for you since she first arrived. See, Amelia, your grandson has come to visit you. Isn't that nice?"

Grandma's face was expressionless.

"I'm just putting Amelia's shoes on, and then she'll be ready. Would you like to walk her to the cafeteria for breakfast?" she asked Horace.

"Okay," he answered hesitantly.

His mom gave him a nudge. "Don't be afraid."

He had never been afraid of his grandma before, but this place was different, with all its strange sounds and smells.

He carefully walked over to the bed and held out his arm.

His mom smiled. "I'm going to help clean up her room."

"Okay," he said again.

Horace began walking slowly, his grandmother by his side. Other residents were coming out of their rooms now too. Horace gently guided his grandma to the dining hall full of folding tables and up to one of the place settings. She sat down and Horace joined her.

"Look, Grandma, your favorite." Horace took a fork and stuck a big piece of toast on the end. "Here, try some." He started to lift it up to her mouth when suddenly she stopped him.

"I'm not a vegetable, Horace. I can do it myself."

To his surprise, she grabbed the utensil and began eating.

She ate a few more bites and then looked thoughtfully at Horace. "What's the matter?" she asked. If her actions hadn't caught him totally off guard, her question did. She looked so different in the nursing home and she'd been so quiet since he'd first arrived, he honestly hadn't thought she'd noticed what was going on around her. "Go ahead," she prodded.

Horace spoke his next words so quickly, his tongue almost tripped over his sentences. "Grandma, you were right! The beetle was a key to a door in the tree! It led to Ancient Egypt! My friends and I saved King Tut, and we discovered the Benben Stone there!"

Despite Horace's excitement, his grandma remained calm. "Shhhhh, Horace," she said softly. "Listen, take a deep breath. You must quiet down." She leaned in closer. "This war is far older than either you or I can imagine, and it will not be won in a single battle." She placed her fork on the plate. "I learned a thing or two watching your grandpa and the Time Keepers over the years."

"You know about the Order?" For weeks Horace had longed to know more about this mysterious group Herman kept referring to.

"Yes, yes. The Order, the highest initiates of the Temple of the Phoenix, the ones in charge of the calendars and, of course, guarding the keystone."

"The keystone? The beetle?"

She laughed as if Horace had said something funny. "There are more sacred stones than I can count. Your beetle is one. But the keystone is the Benben Stone." Grandma paused to let Horace catch up, and then she continued.

"Did you know Akhenaten created your beetle so he could use the Benben Stone as a source of abundance and wealth for the whole country? He wanted to share the secrets of the past with everyone, not just those initiated into the temple. But after Akhenaten's death, the Keepers realized the power of the Benben Stone would be too dangerous if it fell into the wrong hands, and they gave Grandpa the responsibility of caring for both stones."

"But, Grandma, my friends told me Grandpa was caught up in the Michigan Relics, that he made a whole museum exhibit about them. But they turned out to be nothing more than a hoax."

She started to laugh again. "My goodness, your friends aren't wrong, but they can't see beyond the surface of the matter, like so many others. How else could you cover up the appearance of a five-thousand-year-old stone from Egypt or the arrival of a magic scarab beetle in a small town in Michigan? Grandpa made a fake exhibit to hide the stone. Think about it, Horace. Who would look for a magical stone in a museum in Niles?"

Horace flashed back to the newspaper clipping he'd

found in his book on Egypt.

She went on, "So he displayed the Benben Stone in the middle of the museum as one of the prized Michigan Relics. Everyone thought he was nuts. And he was! It was just enough to keep the museum open and to keep away anyone who might have a real interest in these things."

"But, Grandma, if the stone was safe in the museum, how did Smenk get it back?"

She was silent.

A tear started to form in his eye. "Grandma, I know. That's why Smenk killed Grandpa." Horace's mind flashed to the images he'd seen in the stone.

She gripped his small shoulders with her hands and looked him square in the face. "Horace, your grandpa believed in you, and I believe in you." She reached into her pocket. "Here, I've been holding this. He wanted you to have it. I just don't think he ever imagined you'd be reading it so young."

She slipped a small crumpled envelope into his hand. He slid his finger under the flap and opened the letter.

To Horace,

If you are reading this, I imagine you've now discovered who I am, and you've also learned who you are. You were born with a great gift, a gift that has run through our family for generations. It's not a gift available to everyone, though. It has skipped through our family like a pebble on water. Your great-grandmother had the gift, I carried it, and, when you were born, it became clear you possessed it as well.

With this gift, you have the ability to access the true treasure of the past: memory. But not just the memories of stories or everyday events. You can know the memories and histories of civilizations long forgotten, the stories that will help us all truly understand who we are. And the scarab beetle I bequeath to you, while very powerful, is only a tool that magnifies the power you possess. You are the real key, Horace. You are a Time Keeper.

Remember, though, the past is fragile, like a delicate flower. There are many who seek to manipulate our collective memory and others who will try to destroy it altogether. As a Keeper, it is your job not only to guard the memories from these evil forces, but also to share what you discover with the world. The Benben Stone and its knowledge are not meant to be locked in temples or hoarded by powerful rulers; the stone contains a history that must be told. Use the beetle to discover that history and, with it, open an ancient path connecting all of us back to the stars.

Forever your grandpa,

Flinders j. Peabody

Horace felt a tear run down his face.

"There's more," his grandma said encouragingly.

Horace turned the paper over but didn't see anything else. He looked questioningly at Grandma. And then Horace noticed something he'd never noticed before. There between his grandfather's first and last names was the mysterious *j*.

"Grandma, Grandpa also had a *j* for his middle initial?"

She smiled. "That's not a *j*, Horace. Here." She pulled a pen out of her pocket and began to draw a series of shapes.

It was the symbol on the seal of the letter Herman had first brought him; it was the symbol on the back of the beetle; and, he saw now, it was the symbol in his middle initial. "What is it, Grandma?"

"The symbol of the Time Keepers. It's the eye of Horus, your namesake. The beetle is part of your destiny. And it's always been a part of your name."

a note from the author

So much of the inspiration for this story is based on historical facts. The characters, the places, the names, and even many of the objects are real. I've always been drawn to the mysteries of history, and surprisingly, both Egypt and Michigan are full of them.

Horace's name (which is also the name I gave my favorite stuffed animal as a kid) is connected to an Egyptian god and a famous resident in Niles, Michigan. Niles is a real town in the southwest of the state. It has a fascinating past dating to the early frontier first settled by the French. In the nineteenth century it was also an important stop on the Underground Railroad. An old museum called the Chapin House sits in the center of Niles, and houses many bizarre artifacts, including a two-headed sheep.

Although the Michigan Relics never made their way to Niles, they were a real and unexplained collection of objects found in the state in 1890.

The Egyptian artifacts and history mentioned in the story are real as well. The Benben Stone can be traced to the city of Heliopolis, where it was guarded by an order of priests known as the Keepers of Time. The whereabouts of the stone remain a mystery, as does the location of Akhenaten's burial site. Akhenaten and his city, Amarna, dramatically transformed three thousand years of Egyptian history before he died mysteriously, disappearing along with his city from the history books. The lost period of Amarna was only rediscovered in 1922, when Howard Carter stumbled upon King Tut's sealed tomb in the Valley of the Kings. The discoveries inside opened a window into a period of previously forgotten history. One of the discoveries, which left many Egyptologists bewildered by its beauty, was a blue scarab beetle.

acknowledgments

I first shared my ideas for this story with my wife in a New York City taxicab six years ago. Without her support and encouragement, Horace probably would have never made it past Fifty-Seventh Street. But there were many others along the way who have also lent a helping hand. Elizabeth and Abbey, two voracious young readers who constantly badgered me about finishing the story. My sister-in-law, Ashley, who went through an early version of the manuscript chapter by chapter. My friend Jen and in-laws Marie and Len, who provided constant enthusiasm and encouragement. Sophie, a copyreader of sorts, who provided some amazing line-by-line feedback. My agent, Clelia, who worked tirelessly to find a home for Horace. My editor, Catherine, who patiently worked with me to make the narrative clear and strong. Barb, Heather, and everyone at Sleeping Bear who helped bring this story to life. And my parents, who have always supported me unconditionally, no matter the endeavor. Great stories need great families, and I've been lucky to have found one in Sleeping Bear.

about the author

William (Bill) Meyer is an author, teacher, and student of history. He was born in Detroit, and currently lives with his wife in New York, where he is finishing his PhD at New York University and teaching his high-school students about the mysteries of Ancient Egypt.